tulip

To Elisie,

First, I want you to know that I love you. You are such a wonderful person. Thank you for supporting me.

Love
Auntie Mary

MARY E. CHAMBERS

Published by
Mynd Matters Publishing
715 Peachtree Street NE, Suites 100 & 200
Atlanta, GA 30308
www.myndmatterspublishing.com

ISBN-13: 978-1-948145-33-6
E-ISBN: 978-1-948145-37-4

FIRST EDITION

Dedicated with Love
To Mable C. Smith, my grandmother, my mother, my love.

Contents

Prelude 9

Chapter 1: Mama is Dying 11

Chapter 2: Alone and Afraid 15

Chapter 3: Awakening Hell on Earth.................................18

Chapter 4: N—r Girl 30

Chapter 5: Life, Dreams, Reality 33

Chapter 6: A Desolate Field of Flowers............................40

Chapter 7: Cuffed and Chained 49

Chapter 8: The Great Escape 52

Chapter 9: Such Strange Relations 63

Chapter 10: Going Nowhere Fast......................................69

Chapter 11: The Beginning 73

Chapter 12: Malcolm 77

Chapter 13: Wounded by Fate...81

Chapter 14: Saying Goodbye 85

Chapter 15: To the Dearly Departed.................................92

Chapter 16: Love by Another Name................................100

Chapter 17: First Time..107

Chapter 18: Bridge Over Troubled Waters 114

Chapter 19: Helping Hands...119

Chapter 20: Building Together 127

Chapter 21: Courting 132

Chapter 22: Falling in Love 137

Chapter 23: Asking Questions 144

Chapter 24: Happily Ever After 149

Chapter 25: Seeing Ghosts 158

Chapter 26: Solo 166

Chapter 27: Identity 178

Chapter 28: Conflicts and Struggles 185

Chapter 29: Searches of the Heart 192

Special Acknowledgments 205

PRELUDE

I thought it might be a good time to tell you my story—well, sort of my story. It's about my life, and perhaps even a small taste of your life. Our story is also *love*, that universal thing that we all need. Most of us have loved, been loved, or sought love.

This story starts with the birth of Tulip Jameson. Her mother loved flowers, and that was the only flower she knew by name.

Tulip was a breathtaking and beautiful baby girl with rich, earthy brown skin. Her hair was thick, coarse, wavy, and full. She had deep, penetrating brown eyes with perfectly shaped eyebrows. Tulip's face was not quite oval in shape, but its shape flawlessly and subtly framed her features. Her lips were neither thin nor full but perfect all the same. The shape of her nose rose and fell as if born from a deeply-rooted African heritage.

Tulip looked upward to heaven and cried aloud, "Who am I?" She screamed as tears glistened in her dove-shaped eyes.

"*Where do I belong, God?*" she yelled passionately. "I am trying to follow where you are. I am lost and oh, so scared!" Tulip cried a deep bellow from within her stomach. The year was 1910 and she was only twelve years old. She knew she would soon have to face this world alone, without the warmth, love, and comfort of Mama.

chapter one

Mama is Dying

"Mama, Mama, you're sick," Tulip murmured as she stroked the older woman's rough, dry, and cracked black hands. Mama's hands showed years of labor, pain, loss, and lack of love.

Tears formed in the corner of Mama's vacant, aged gray eyes. Her eyes were almost translucent. It was as though the angels of death waited for her. Mama knew that the time was near for her sad hard, and short life to end. She was not an old woman, but the years had taken their toll and made her appear older than she was. The long days working in the sun had wrinkled her face and the worry of providing for her baby girl had prematurely whitened her hair. Her hands were rough and hard from digging food out of the hard ground and washing clothes. Her only fear was that she had to leave her beautiful, young girl alone in this cruel man's world.

Mama coughed long and hard as beads of sweat formed on her brow. Tulip tried the best she could to console her.

"Here, Mama, let me make you some tea," Tulip said softly and lovingly. "I'll make you some hot sweet tea, Mama. Just the way you like it."

Tulip knew that there was no sugar cane for tea, and just a few grains of tealeaves left in the can. She looked around the dimly lit shack like she expected to see the cupboards magically fill with food and pots brim with meat and potatoes on the stove. The shack was one large room with a makeshift bed in one corner and a wood-burning stove in the other. It was dirty, old, and devoid of God's sunlight. Every day was dank, cold, and gray. It was the only home that Tulip and Mama knew.

"Make some tea, baby," Mama said, wincing in pain. "Yo' Mama sick. I got real bad sicknesses, sugar," she whispered as aches attacked every muscle in her tired, young body. Even whispering required faith in God as she forced her body to muscle words from her mouth. "Tulip, yo' Mama is dying," she said. Her voice was full of shame, sadness, and regret.

Mama was not a bad-looking woman. She would have been considered fair. Her skin was a rich, black hue, like that of coal. Though it glistened in the sun, it was scarred from years of poverty, abuse, and hard living.

While Tulip's maternal grandparents Big Paw and Big Maw were slaves, Mama was born free and lived with her parents until she was sent away at the age of seven to work in the fields. Mama was not stupid and had common sense, even though she had had very little schooling.

Like many poor Negro girls, Mama had been sexually abused, beaten, neglected, and abandoned since birth. But Mama was a strong woman with deep faith. She was only nine years old the first time she was raped. At the time, it was the white man who owned the land where her parents worked. Over the years, many more would follow. Some were black, some were strangers, and some were related by blood—even her own Papa. Now, at twenty-four, she was dying. Too many violations to remember. Some memories are best left forgotten.

Mama was the only family that Tulip had. She didn't have any siblings, or even a Papa to speak of. Many men visited Mama, but none was said to be her Papa. Mama never spoke of her family and Tulip never asked. They lived together in a one-room shack located in rural Hartford, Connecticut during the cold winter of 1922.

Tulip began to pick through the wood to make a fire in the old wood-burning stove for Mama's tea. She noticed that the woodpile was getting low. She and Mama had gathered as much wood as they could before Mama took to her bed with sickness. Tulip knew she'd soon have go out into the cold to gather more, but she didn't want to leave Mama alone.

Tulip stuck a piece of wood in the old stove to make a little fire, as Mama had shown her. She made sure she didn't catch fire as the flames leaped from the stove like a devil reaching out for her soul. She was careful not to place too much wood inside the stove since she knew what was left had to last a while. She would only use the precious kindling as needed. At that critical time, wood was definitely needed.

The fire immediately spread warmth throughout the small shack. Tulip stood gazing into the flames. They were pretty, in an odd sort of way, and the cracking noises were like music to her ears. For a moment, she was lost deep inside the blaze. Mama's raspy cough broke the moment of pleasure.

Standing at the stove, Tulip carefully warmed some of the remaining water from a rusty pot. She hoped Mama wouldn't notice that the tea wasn't sweet. Once the steam rose from the pot, Tulip slowly poured the water into a small bowl with the last of the tea leaves, being careful not to spill it or burn her hands. She stirred the leaves in a circular motion until the water went from being clear to a foggy green.

Tulip lifted the tea-filled bowl and let some of the warm, weak green tea slip through her perfectly shaped small lips. The tea was strong and bitter. Tulip frowned with disgust. "Nasty," she said aloud.

Tulip gently walked to the side of the bed where Mama lay dying. "Here, Mama, I made you some tea. Just the way you like it."

Tulip placed the bowl of green tea on the dirt floor so she could lift Mama's head up to drink the bitter brew.

"Here, Mama, drink a little," Tulip said sweetly.

Mama was so weak it was hard to hold her steady to drink the tea. As Tulip reached to help balance Mama, the bowl of tea slipped from her hand and down to the dirt floor, splattering across Tulip's dirty feet. Tulip shrieked from the burn of the hot liquid.

She laid Mama back down and began to cry.

chapter two

Alone and Afraid

*A*s night fell, the winter winds blew hard outside of the one-room shack. Tulip carefully lit a small candle using the fire from the stove. Without the faint glow, the shack would be pitch dark. Tulip was afraid of what lurked in the darkness.

The cold harsh winter wind made its way into their shack and Tulip shivered from the frigid air. She had placed all the blankets and old rags upon Mama to keep her warm. Tulip knew that Mama needed more than the few old blankets, rags, and a pot of weak tea to get better, but there was nothing in that dark old room called "home."

"Tulip! Tulip, come here, Sugar," Mama whispered hoarsely, with a sense of urgency in her dying voice.

Mama always called her only daughter "Sugar" because her baby girl was the sweetest thing in the world. Tulip brought happiness to her otherwise bleak world and always made her smile. Just like a sweet lil' thing, Tulip was Sugar.

To Mama, Tulip was a thing of beauty, inside and out. Tulip's features were so delicate that she always looked like she would break if held too tightly. Tulip's skin was flawless and she had eyes as dark as night, but holding a soft kindness. For her fourteen years, Tulip's body was beginning to take a woman's form: a small waist, wide hips, pointed breasts, a round butt, and shapely legs. Mama knew that in time, Tulip would have to fend off touchy, greedy hands. She had managed to keep Tulip safe from unwanted hands and would often hide Tulip when strangers would come to the shack for one reason or another. She now regretted never telling Tulip about men who may hurt her or treat her cruelly for no reason other than being a girl.

She never told Tulip that people would treat her differently because of the color of her skin. How do you tell a child never to trust and how to be afraid? Mama only told her one and only daughter to trust in God, pray, be clean, remember her manners, treat old people with respect, and never beg for food or money.

As Mama struggled to call out to Tulip, Tulip slowly walked over to her. Mama reached for her with shaking hands,. Tulip looked into Mama's dying eyes and wondered at what moment they had turned from a beautiful, kind brown to a weak, sad gray. Mama smiled as if she knew what her baby girl was thinking. With that smile on her face, her head slowly drifted back into Tulip's arms.

Tulip felt the weight of Mama's body. It was getting too heavy to hold. Tulip slowly let Mama's body sink into the sheetless, makeshift hay bed. Mama's eyes stared straight ahead, as if she was looking at something other than Tulip. *How odd,* Tulip thought to herself.

"Mama, Mama," Tulip quietly called, as tears formed in her frightened eyes. Tulip lifted Mama's hand, but it slowly fell back onto the crude hay pallet. Tulip began to gently shake Mama's shoulders, but Mama's body did not respond. Tulip began to shake her more forcefully while calling out to her, but Mama's body moved lifelessly. Tulip turned Mama's face toward her so she could look into her now dull, gray eyes. Mama's eyes were open, but no sign of life stared back at her.

Tulip had never been around dead people. She had seen dead dogs, birds, rats, mice, cats, rabbits, and farm animals, but never a human. In fact, Tulip had never been to a funeral.

Is my Mama dead? Fear gripped her body. Tulip struggled to catch her breath as a warm rush flooded her body. The fire in the stove was out and the cold wind entered through every crack of the one-room shack, but she still felt a warmth take over her body. Like raindrops from heaven, beads of sweat and tears joined together and rolled down Tulip's face until they eventually showered Mama, as well.

Tulip stood tall and looked down upon the lifeless body before her. She gazed at her dead Mama until the candle's flame died, allowing her to look no more. A small trickle of fluid flowed down from her Secret and past her knees until it finally rested on the floor beneath her feet. Mama was dead, and Tulip was reborn a woman.

chapter three

Awakening Hell on Earth

*T*ulip arrived in the state of New York in the cold winter of 1925. It was a long, hard way from rural Connecticut. Tulip could not believe that three years had passed since Mama had died.

After Mama's death Tulip had stayed in the shack with Mama's dead body until she could no longer stand the smell. Tulip slept in the makeshift hay bed with Mama. She found sleep hard to come by with Mama's body being so hard and cold. Eventually she could no longer bear the smell. As time passed, there was no wood for the fire, no candles for light, no water to drink, and no food to eat. Tulip hated to leave Mama all alone in that old, dark one-room shack. But she was cold and hungry. She also feared she was dying because she could not stop the blood from coming down her legs. But where would she go if she left the shack?

Tulip recalled that sometimes Mama talked about the Barnesville Plantation where she was born. Her Mama and Papa and other family had worked there. She always told Tulip that if something ever happened to her, Tulip had to find her way to the Barnesville Plantation in the state of Maryland, and maybe, she would find her kinfolk.

Tulip had no money, no food, and few clothes to protect her from the harsh winter weather. But what choice did she have? Surely if she stayed in the ramshackle room, she would die, like Mama.

Tulip gathered her courage and left the shack she called home. First, she picked through her meager clothing, which mostly consisted of rags. She put on as many as possible. She wrapped some of the remaining rags around her waist and between her legs to try to stop the bleeding from her Secret. She wanted to kiss Mama goodbye, but the smell was too bad for her to get close. She instead offered a poem:

Here lays my Mama who was a God-fearing good woman and
who committed no sins;
Here lays my Mama, who gave me life and took care of me like a
rooster protects her little hen;
Here lays my Mama, who is now dust in the wind;
Here lays my Mama, who now with her God and her other kin;
Here lays my Mama. She was my only friend and
I will love her until my end.

Like a new baby bird leaving the nest, Tulip walked out with a heavy heart, but never looked back.

For a few days, Tulip skipped along the road, dragging her belongings. She had walked these roads on many occasions with Mama in search of work. She nibbled on hard bread and picked berries from the vines. Nights were the scariest because she was afraid of snakes and noises in the woods. Sometimes she would sing out loud or just pray. Mama had told her that praying to God would keep the bad things away. In their travels Mama had taught her not to sleep on the open roads, so Tulip was careful to heed this advice for fear that some bad person may hurt her. She wondered how far away Maryland was.

One morning, as she was walking along, tired and lonely, Tulip heard the sound of an approaching buggy behind her. Tulip moved to the side of the road to let the buggy pass. A few wagons and buggies had passed her but none ever stopped to offer her a ride.

When the buggy passed by Tulip, she could not help but notice the nicely dressed man driving the horses. He smiled as he passed her and continued on down the road. But then the buggy stopped.

Tulip didn't move. The man turned to get a better look at the unkempt little creature. She was a poor sight—dirty and ragged, with hair every which way on her head. She resembled a bag of bones. *She's either on her own or heading home,* he thought to himself.

"Hey girl, where you headed?"

Taken aback by the man addressing her, Tulip hesitated for what seemed like forever. She then replied, "Maryland."

This got the man's attention. "Did I hear you correctly—Maryland?" He chuckled. "Where is your Mama?"

"Dead," replied Tulip as she kicked at the dirt. She rocked back and forth, with her head downcast. Tulip started to scratch at her skin from the many bug bites.

The man looked at Tulip. "Sorry for the loss of your Mama. I know that she is in heaven with God. Now, little Miss, judging from all that scratching, you may need a bath before you get to Maryland. You are welcome to come to my home where my wife can give you a good bath. I am sure you could also use a good meal before you continue on your way to Maryland."

The man watched as Tulip tried to decide. "Come on now, make up your mind. It's Sunday and I got a sermon to preach. If you're not coming, I'll leave you be and I will be on my way."

"You're a preacher!" Tulip suddenly burst out loudly.

"Yes, lil' lady, I am" replied the man.

Tulip recalled how Mama had told her to place her trust in only God and the preacher. With that, Tulip gathered her sack of belongings in her arms and ran to the wagon as fast as she could.

Preacher Copeland oversaw a small African Methodist church in rural Connecticut. He and his wife June had seven kids: four boys and three girls. The church members had all worked together to build a home for his large family, down the road from his church.

As Preacher Copeland pulled the buggy closer toward the house, Tulip noticed children sitting on the ground. Each looked down at a book in his or her hands. When they heard the buggy approaching, they looked up but didn't move, smile, or offer any greetings. They just stared and showed no emotion.

"Mother, I home!" Preacher Copeland called out.

The front door to the freshly painted white and blue A-framed house swung open and out came a large, colored woman with big breasts. She was much taller than Preacher Copeland, who was rather short in stature and had curly hair and a nice face. On the other hand, Misses Copeland was not very attractive, and looked mean.

Misses Copeland looked Tulip up and down and frowned. "Now who have you brought home?" she asked, with her hands resting on her thick waist. "I know not another mouth to feed," she added, shaking her wrapped head from side to side.

"This here is little motherless Tulip. Her Mama died and she on her way to good 'ol Maryland to find her kin. Since Maryland is such a long way, I thought the Godly thing to do was for us to help God's creature before she makes such a long journey," Preacher Copeland replied, winking and smiling at his wife.

"What foolishness, walking to Maryland! Stupid, silly child. She's probably a throw-away like the rest of the ungrateful bunch," she muttered, looking in the direction of the children. They quickly buried their heads in their books. "Well, she's a dirty little thing. She needs washing before she comes in the house. She probably stinks and is bug-infested. Have her sit over there with the other children until they finish their Bible study and then I'll have Maggie to help her get washed and changed out of those rags," she said angrily. "What did you call her?"

"Tulip," said Preacher Copeland.

Misses Copeland turned toward the house while mumbling to herself, "Ain't Tulip the name of a flower? What a sinful way to shame God's gift to His creations, by wasting the name on a n—r girl." She stomped back into the house with a slight bend in her back and slammed the door, causing the children to jump in fear.

Preacher Copeland told Tulip to go sit with the other children and instructed his daughter Maggie (who was not really his daughter) to get her washed up.

<hr />

It had been two years since Tulip arrived at the Copelands', and life had not been easy. Tulip learned that all the children were either runaways or given to Copelands. Each child had assigned work to do in the house and at church. When they were not working, they had to read the Bible. Then they had to kneel and pray. While they received three meals a day, the food was not very hearty or filling. Usually, it was just beans and bread.

Tulip was often very hungry. She longed for some of the food that she saw Preacher Copeland and his wife eat: fried chicken, greens, potatoes, and corn bread. However, asking for, or—even worse—stealing food would earn you a beating in front the whole church congregation, and no food for a week.

Tulip wanted to leave and continue on her trip to find her kin in Maryland. One time, she told Preacher Copeland that she really needed to be on her way. He marched her to the front of the congregation and told them how ungrateful she was after they had opened their home to her. Misses Copeland whipped her so hard, she couldn't sit for a week. That night, Tulip cried for her Mama.

Many nights, she would hear the other children crying, as well, especially Maggie, after Maggie's prayer time alone with Preacher Copeland. Maggie told Tulip that soon, she would have to pray with Preacher Copeland at night. Tulip didn't quite understand, but she knew that it was not something she wanted to do.

The church was having a big revival and colored folks were coming from all over—some as far as New York. All the children had to work hard to prepare food, clean the church, and wash and scrub floors. Misses Copeland had dresses made for the girls to wear to the revival. This was the first decent dress Tulip had since arriving at the Copelands.

During the revival, folks were taken to the river to be baptized. Tulip and a few of the other kids were told to stay at the church and set out the food for when the congregation returned. This was the first time in two years that both Copelands were away together. Tulip was elated.

As Tulip was setting out the food, she heard a man and his wife telling Preacher Copeland that they would not be joining them at the river. Preacher Copeland agreed that this was acceptable, because they were already saved, but insisted that the couple sit down for a decent meal before their departure. Tulip watched as the man and woman packed up their buggy. They returned and sat down for a meal.

Tulip don't know where she got the idea, but she ran back to the house and reached under the bed that she shared with the other girls and found her sack. She was moving so fast, she was shaking. She went into the kitchen and grabbed some biscuits and meat and wrapped the food in paper. She then looked out front the door. No one was around.

Tulip walked back to the church, being careful not to draw any attention to herself. She noticed the couple standing there, shaking other people's hands. Tulip ran back to where their horse and buggy was tied. She jumped up onto the back of the wagon and slipped under the covering. It was hot and smelly, but it would do. Tulip's heart was beating fast. She knew that the Copelands would put the worst whooping on her, or even kill her. But she had to go.

Finally, Tulip heard laughing, and someone got on the buggy. She said a silent prayer, and off they went.

The man and woman stopped a few times to retrieve things from the back of the wagon, but they never discovered Tulip. When Tulip had to pee, she would just lie on her back, pull down her bloomers, and relieve herself. The pee would just fall through the cracks of the wagon bed. Her back ached. Sometimes, she was able to stretch out when she knew the man and woman were away from the buggy. The man and woman talked and laughed a lot. They seemed happy.

After several days of travelling, the wagon made its final stop. The man nudged his wife, waking her to tell her they had made it home. Tulip overheard the man tell his wife that it was so late, he would empty the buggy in the morning. When it was quiet, Tulip came out from underneath the covering.

Along her journey, Tulip found that the nights were lonely,

scary, and long. She recalled her travels on various roads with Mama. If night fell before they reached home, Tulip and Mama would always leave the road and find a creek or large tree to sleep beside. Mama said that this would keep them safe at night from wild animals and bad people. During the day, Tulip would pick fruit from the trees or berries from the vines, like she did with Mama. She ate wild mint to stop the rumbling in her stomach. She drank water from the rivers and streams. It was too cold to remove all her clothing and bathe, but she did manage to wash in small streams, removing only what was necessary.

Tulip didn't know where she was walking. She just walked. Sometimes, she would get rides on hay wagons with strangers, but she was careful to stay near the very back, just in case she had to jump off and run. Sometimes a stranger would give her a little food and a piece of extra clothing, concerned that she would freeze to death. She would tell the people she met that she was on an errand for her Mama, and would always ask if she was going the right way for Maryland. Often, strangers would laugh and tell her that she had a long way to go.

When Tulip saw a farm with children, she watched the children play and wished she could play with them. In her loneliness and desperation for a little pleasure, Tulip would sometimes approach the children, but they would run in fear because she was so dirty. Other times, they threw rocks at her to make her run away.

One day, when she approached a farmhouse, the children ran in fear to get their Mama. Tulip was so tired and hungry that she just sat down on the ground. Their Mama, a woman with hair so yellow it could have been gold, approached Tulip. Tulip looked into her blue eyes. She had never seen blue eyes before. *How pretty*, she thought.

"Who are you, child?" the Mama asked. "Where's your Mama? Are you hurt? Come in the house with me, child, so that I can clean you up and get a better look at you," the children's Mama commanded, but not in a mean way.

"Who is she, Mama?" the children questioned. "Is she dying?"

"She's so dirty! Look at her feet, Mama, blood! Mama, blood!" the children yelled.

Even though the children were just as dirty, they found Tulip detestable.

"She a n——r girl, Mama," the children said in unison. "Mama, Papa don't want no n——rs in the house," they said, with a little fear and concern for their Mama.

"Get!" the Mama screamed at the children, who were a little younger than Tulip. "You, John Jr.! Come help me carry her into the house."

John Jr. was very fearful and knew that his Papa would be mad, but he had to obey his Mama. Even though this girl was a n——r, she needed help, and God said to help those in need. John Jr. and his Mama carried poor, dirty little Tulip into the house.

Tulip allowed herself to be lifted. She was just too tired and weak to resist. Plus, this golden-haired lady looked like one of the angels in her Mama's Bible. *This must be heaven*, Tulip thought as she looked around. *Did I die? 'Cause there's a golden-haired lady and this house is so pretty.* There was a room with a table and chairs and flowers on the table. The house had real glass windows framed by pretty, ruffled yellow curtains. There was no makeshift bed in the middle of the room. There was even a hard floor with no dirt.

The house smelled good and felt warm. Tulip's stomach growled from the different aromas coming from the kitchen, where there were fresh biscuits baking and meat cooking. Tulip yearned to ask for something to eat, but she remembered that her Mama had told her not to beg. The golden-haired lady told Tulip to sit on the floor because she was too dirty to sit on the sofa. Tulip didn't really know what a sofa was, so she was ready to sit on the floor.

The other children had come back into the house and had gathered around to look at this dirty n—r girl. No n—r had ever been in their house.

Tulip slowly looked at the children. Some looked like the golden-haired lady and some looked a little different, with brown and black hair. There were a least four or five, Tulip thought, as many children as fingers on her one hand. Their Mama led Tulip into another room, where the biggest bucket Tulip had ever seen stood in the middle. She gave each of the children smaller buckets and told them fetch some water from the well. She then told Tulip to take off her clothes.

Tulip could not imagine exposing her naked bottom to a complete stranger. She just sat on the floor, motionless. The children came back towing full buckets of water. Their Mama poured each into the big bucket in the middle of the room. She told Tulip again— a little more forcefully this time—to take off her clothes, as she poured hot water from the kettle off the wood burning stove into the big bucket, which she called a tub. She told the children to fetch some more cool water from the well.

John Jr. looked at his Mama. "But she's a n—r, Mama. She can't bathe in our tub."

The golden-haired lady walked right up to John Jr. and asked him if he remembered the Bible story of Jesus washing the feet of a poor woman. John Jr. hung his head and nodded to his Mama. No other explanation was need.

Tulip stood very still. She didn't want the Mama, with her

golden blond hair and bluest eyes, to see her private parts.

The Mama seemed to understand, and left the room. When she returned, she put a large sheet around Tulip. "Now," she said, "Take off your clothes in private."

Tulip had never had a bath in a big tub before. She sat naked in the tub with her knees drawn close to her slightly formed breasts in fear. She never spoke a word. The Mama began to wash her, while pouring soothing, clear water into the tub. It felt so good that Tulip slowly began to release her knees from her chest. The Mama smiled while her children laughed and pointed at Tulip through the window, though still fearful that their Papa would find out that the n—r girl was in the house and had bathed in the big tub.

The Mama gave Tulip some clean clothes because Tulip's own clothes were burned in the wood burning stove. Tulip even had some underwear to put on to cover her private parts. They looked funny, but felt nice. Tulip thought about how nice the underwear was, and how clean she felt. With eyes cast downwards, Tulip simply said, "Thank you Ma'am."

Sensing that her husband would be home soon, for the first time, a little fear crept into the Mama's belly. She gave Tulip a knapsack with a few pieces of bread and meat. She didn't ask Tulip any more questions. She led Tulip into the barn and told her to rest until the morning, before she continued on her journey. She told Tulip not to come out of the barn under any circumstance until morning, and then to leave immediately. She told Tulip that her husband may not take kindly to Tulip if he found her there, and with that, she closed the barn door.

Tulip found a small corner in the barn and took a seat. She looked around the barn at the tools and hay. The barn had a musty odor, but it was not too bad, and it was better than her old home.

Tulip could hear the children laughing and playing outside. She peeked through a crack in the barn and saw one girl who had golden hair like her Mama, playing with doll who had golden hair. Tulip thought, *I've never had a doll.*

In that instance, Tulip's stomach called out to her with a loud rumble. Realizing that she was hungry, Tulip opened the knapsack that the Mama had given her and started to eat pieces of meat and bread. It was so good that she wanted to eat it all, but she knew she needed to save some. The meat was salty, and she wanted water, but she remembered what the children's Mama had told her. *How nice and pretty their Mama was*, Tulip thought to herself. Was her Mama pretty? She was nice, but not pretty and golden.

Tulip began to cry, "I want my Mama! I want my Mama!" She cried hard, but quietly, because she did not want the Mama to think that Tulip was not grateful for her kindness. Eventually, Tulip was engulfed with sleep.

chapter four

N—r Girl

"Look! Look! She is still in there," the children said as they opened the door of the barn. Tulip was asleep.

"Do you think she's dead?" asked the youngest of the Betts children.

"No, stupid," John Jr. said.

"Don't call me stupid. Mama said name-calling is a sin!" the youngest child yelled at his big brother.

"Shut up, both of you," whispered one girl, a head shorter than John Jr. Her golden hair and blue eyes were like her Mama's. "We'll wake her up."

"So what?" said John Jr., who was thirteen years old and tall for his age, with dark hair and brown eyes like his Papa. "She's a n—r. Papa said n—rs are as bad as the devil. N—s ain't human, and white people must stay away from them," he proudly stated.

"But the Bible says that all people are created in the form of God," said the girl who looked like their Mama.

"Except *n—rs!*" screamed John Jr.

"But Mama said to be nice to her!" protested the youngest child.

"Look, it's moving," the middle girl said. She looked like her big brother, John Jr.

Ignoring their Mama's orders, the Betts children crept into the barn one by one to get a better look at Tulip, with John Jr. leading the way.

"See, I told you she was not dead," said John Jr.

"She looks better all cleaned up," said the young girl who looked like her Mama.

"She could be pretty if she wasn't a n—r," the youngest child said softly.

"But she's a stinky *n—r!*" John Jr. started angrily at his siblings. "And don't you forget it."

Lost in the best sleep she had had in the past year, Tulip could faintly hear the rumblings of the Betts children. She was lost in a beautiful dream about a field full of flowers and tulips of all colors. As she skipped toward the field, their perfume filled her nostrils. Birds were singing, and she hummed:

The fields of warmth are drawing me near,
can it be that this is not a dream?
Heaven's stairway is lined with silver and gold,
but my field is scented with
Life's meaning of love;
I am swept away in this moment of joy,
so overjoyed I can only wonder
If it is possible to be more...

Tulip! Tulip! Someone was calling her name. She looked around but saw no one there. The scent of flowers was so intoxicating that they made Tulip want to lie down and sleep—but that voice sounded so familiar. *Tulip! Tulip, come, Sugar.*

Suddenly, Tulip knew who was calling. She sprang to her feet and yelled, "Mama!"

The Betts children all jumped in fright, as if they had heard the roar of a wild beast. Their eyes grew wide as they watched Tulip slowly open her own eyes and see all of their faces before her.

Tulip was frozen. She was transfixed in both the dream and this new reality. Her heart was pumping hard and fast and her mind was calling *Mama,* but her eyes were fixed on the Betts children, as theirs were fixed on her.

Suddenly, the old barn door opened, and there stood Papa Betts, a big, hairy, mean-looking man. His face was red, and his hands were as dirty as his clothes. His skin was rough and hard from working long days in the sun and his body reeked of a foul smell—a combination of not bathing and daily consumption of hard liquor. Papa Betts's eyes had no joy. They did not blink, and were transfixed on Tulip. He hated his life, but even more, he hated those lazy, no-account n—rs.

chapter five

Life, Dreams, Reality

The Betts Farm had once been prosperous and the talk of the town. Papa Betts's father had inherited the Betts Farm from his own father, who owned slaves to work the fields. After the end of slavery and the Civil War, the n—rs wanted their freedom and ran off the farm, leaving the Betts clan to fend for themselves. With no slaves to work the fields, the Betts Farm fell into hard times, and eventually, all was lost. After emancipation, many former slaves were able to buy land and operate their own farms. While Papa Betts watched n—rs prosper, he saw his own father drink himself to death, and his mother die destitute. The Betts family was now poor white trash, and Papa Betts had inherited a broken down, worthless farm, along with a deep-rooted hatred for all n—rs.

"What the hell is all of this ruckus?" belted Papa Betts.

"Look, Papa," John Jr. said, pointing excitedly at Tulip. "It's a n—r!"

At the sound of the word n—r, Papa Betts forcibly pushed the children out of the way, nearly knocking the youngest child to the barn's hard, dirty floor. Full of rage, Papa Betts was ready to beat the hell out of this n—r who was invading his property and home.

"Boy," he yelled to John Jr., "get my gun, and don't let no dust settle on your lazy ass."

"Yes, sir," John Jr. replied shakily as he ran off to fetch his Papa's gun, nearly taking the barn door with him. Chickens scattered and fretted as he ran by.

As the other Betts children parted to make way for their Papa, their faces were full of fear for themselves and, understandably, fear for Tulip. Even though she was a n—r, they knew Papa Betts's rage, and Tulip was only a child, like them.

"There," the Betts children pointed nervously at Tulip as she lay helpless on the cold, hard, dirty barn floor. Papa Betts looked down and a saw a small bundle shaking before him.

"What in the hell is this?" he asked himself. "Get up, gal!" Papa Betts yelled.

At the command, Tulip leapt to her feet, scared and frightened. Her legs were shaking so badly that she could hardly stand. She dared not look at the man who was saying all kinds of curse words and nasty things to her. *Who is this person?* Tulip thought to herself. *Why is yelling and cursing at me?* The Betts children began to laugh, seeing the fright in Tulip, glad that their Papa's wrath was aimed at someone else instead of them.

"Stop all of that ruckus!" Papa Betts yelled at his children as he slowly and greedily looked Tulip up and down.

John Jr. ran into the house. "Papa wants his gun! He is going to kill that n—r girl," he announced to his Mama.

"John Jr., did you say your Papa is here?" Mama Betts asked. *He wasn't due home until late tomorrow,* she thought.

"Yes, Mama, but I need to hurry. Papa sent me to fetch his gun."

Mama Betts dropped the knife she had been using to cut carrots and ran from the house, clutching her heart the whole while. Mama Betts had a bad heart. Shortly after arriving in Canton, New York, her family was lost in a fire that burned down their home. Mama

Betts (then known as Karen Isbister) had been away at school, in Boston. Upon learning of her family's tragic fate, she returned to Canton to bury her kin. With little money and no other family to support her at seventeen, when she was considered a grown woman, Karen Isbister found herself in dire straits.

Because news travelled fast, John Betts, who was thirty-seven at the time, heard of the Isbister family tragedy and knew of the surviving daughter: young, educated, beautiful, and possibly a virgin. While he wasn't educated, John Betts wasn't a bad-looking man at the time, and he did inherit his family farm, with still over twenty acres left (one hundred acres were either sold or lost). He was looking to start a family and was in serious need of help to run the Betts Farm. While he had never courted Karen Isbister, he knew that she needed a husband, and that he was the perfect man.

John Betts asked Karen Isbister to marry him. Being alone, afraid, and full of grief, Karen agreed. She didn't have many options, and Betts had land and had helped her with the arrangements for her family's burial. A week after burying her family, Karen Isbister married John Betts in a civil ceremony, and to her dismay, moved into the run-down Betts Farm. Within fourteen years, she had five children: three boys and two girls.

Life was hard on the Betts Farm and John Betts was not a very good provider, nor was he a loving husband or father. Whatever little money Karen had brought to the marriage, John Betts had long since spent on whiskey and women. He ruled his home with fear, bullying, and self-righteousness. Karen loved her children and tried to raise them in a Christian home. She never asked herself if she loved her husband. *What was the point?*

Mama Betts ran into the barn and stopped dead in her tracks. There was Papa Betts, pointing a loaded rifle directly at poor Tulip's small, frightened face.

"Look here what we got, Mama," said Papa Betts. "A n—r wench trying to steal our stuff." He was downright giddy.

"No! No, Papa," Mama Betts said softly, moving gingerly toward Tulip. She was still holding her heart, which was beating rapidly from all the running and the thought of what Papa Betts may do to the child.

"Papa," Mama Betts continued, "silly me, I let this poor lil' child come into the barn to get a little rest. She was tired and hurt. I just wanted her to get a little rest before she continued on her journey."

Papa Betts was still pointing the gun directly at Tulip. Tulip was so frightened of the big, mean white man that she couldn't move. Tulip kept her head down and her eyes fixated on the ground, remembering her Mama's words about white people.

The Betts children were transfixed and wide-eyed as they watched their Papa reach out and yank Tulip up by her hair and pull her close to him. This was the most excitement they had seen in their short lives, and they relished the moment, even though it meant that a child not much older than them was going to endure the torment of Papa Betts. They dared not make a sound. Collectively, they wished they were invisible, for fear that his anger might turn toward them.

Papa Betts's foul odor penetrated Tulip's nostrils. The odor reminded Tulip of a half-eaten animal left to rot in the sun. His teeth were green, yellow, and brown. The whites of his eyes were red, and he had large, bushy, and craggy eyebrows. His face was scarred and covered in hair, including crusty hairs that hung from his nose. His thin lips were lost in the mess of hair that framed his face, matted, tangled, and unkempt. The big hands that lifted Tulip by her hair were bigger than Tulip's face and as dirty as Papa Betts's clothes. To

Tulip, Papa Betts was surely the boogey man, or maybe even the devil.

Between the unimaginable fear and the unbearable bad odor reeking from Papa Betts, Tulip was sure she would either pass out or throw up on his clothes. Given the condition of his clothes, however, this may have been an improvement.

"Is what my wife say true, n——r?" Papa Betts yelled.

Tulip wet herself, the urine slowly creeping from her Secret, down her inner thighs, and reaching her calves and feet. The wetness was warm, providing a slight distraction from the immediate situation. She was wearing the long, clean dress that Mama Betts had given her, however, so no one could see the puddle of pee forming underneath her.

"Yes, sir," Tulip quivered.

It felt like Papa Betts was going to explode. The rage was building and building. He wanted to bash this n——r's face in as hard as he could.

Mama Betts knew that if she didn't make a move soon, Papa Betts was going to hurt this poor child badly. He may even kill her. *Who would care?* With that thought, Mama Betts inched closer to Tulip. She wanted to help, but she knew that if she tried, her husband's wrath would be directed at her, and perhaps even their children. Out of fear for herself and her children, she could only say a small internal prayer for Tulip.

"Yessir, mister man," Tulip managed again, shaking like a leaf falling from a tree.

"What? What was that?" smirked Papa Betts. "*N——r*, I can't hear you!" Spit flew from his mouth as he yelled. Papa Betts was enjoying his newfound power and found it sexually stimulating.

Tulip tried hard to muscle the strength to find her voice, but again, she only managed to mutter, "Yes, master."

Hearing this deeply incensed Papa Betts. His muscled, swollen face reddened, and with one hand, he threw Tulip across the barn. Her small seventy-pound frame crashed against the cold, dirty floor. She screamed in pain and yelled for her Mama.

The children all scattered like a swarm of flies. Mama Betts covered her mouth to prevent any sound. She wanted to move toward Tulip, but her body stood frozen.

"Now you know who's the master!" Papa Betts yelled as he shook his finger at Tulip with a renewed sense of power. He had never had a n—r work for him, as they did when slavery was practiced. Though the n—rs called themselves free, they would never be free in Papa Betts's mind. Even though slavery had long since been abolished and it was illegal to own a slave, Papa Betts thought to himself, *Now I am somebody with my own n—r to work for me. This wench will have many more n—rs to work for me, and I will be rich again, like my Papa and Grandpapa!* A slow smile spread across his thin, hairy, crusted lips. He turned to Mama Betts, who was standing behind him like a statute.

"What are you still doing here?" Papa Betts yelled. "Is my supper ready? Get along and do your chores!" he hammered.

"Do you want me to send the girl on her way?" Mama Betts sheepishly asked, fully aware of the coming answer.

"*No!*" Papa Betts spitted toward his wife. "This here *n—r* stole food from us and kept it in that there knapsack, and I am going to get the law."

Papa Betts knew full well that his wife, with her simple and godly ways, had given Tulip that food, but it was his food, and Tulip was a *n—r*. Furthermore, he had no intention of involving the law. This was his property, and now Tulip was his property.

Mama Betts looked at Tulip's crumpled body. Tulip hadn't moved since Papa Betts had thrown her to the hard dirt floor. She just whimpered like a newborn puppy for her long-dead, poor Mama. As Mama Betts looked at Tulip, she was moved to tears. *She is only a child,* she thought, as she turned to look at Papa Betts. He had a look on his face that made her realize that her husband had some ugly plans in store for the poor little creature, and she felt helpless.

"Get! Get!" Papa yelled at his wife, while keeping his gaze fixed on his newfound possession. With that, Mama Betts slowly and sadly walked out of the barn. Papa Betts calmly added, "And close that door behind you."

chapter six

A Desolate Field of Flowers

*T*ulip lay on the old barn's hard dirt floor. She was fully aware that this horrible man was still in the barn. Her body was cut, bloody, and hurt from being thrown. The pain was unbearable. She only wanted her Mama, and she wished she were dead, too.

Tulip could hear the man moving about the old barn, talking to himself, but she couldn't understand his words. *Maybe*, Tulip thought, *if I just lie here really still, he won't see.* Tulip could feel the warm blood easing from her mouth. Her limbs hurt. As she slowly opened her eyes, she could see the evil man moving about the old barn through the haze. She saw neither the children nor Mama Betts. Tulip thought that if she went to sleep, maybe she could go back to the field of flowers.

Tulip, Tulip, a voice called out.

Tulip felt herself moving across the cold dirt floor of the barn. *Why I am being dragged? I am moving. My arm is hurt.* She could see the field of flowers, especially the many beautiful tulips. *They are so beautiful. Red, white, pink, orange…*

Tulip, Tulip, the voice called.

"That's my Mama!" Tulip happily shouted. "Mama! Mama! I'm here. Where are you, Mama?"

This straw is sticking in my back like sharp little needles, thought

Tulip. *It's getting cold in here. Where are my clothes?* Tulip wondered. Tulip began to panic. *I can't breathe! Something heavy is on my body.*

"*Get off of me!* I can't breathe!" Tulip screamed in terror. Tulip struggled futilely to the point of exhaustion to get the heaviness off of her body.

Tulip, Tulip, the voice called.

"Mama, I can't find you! Where are you?" Tulip cried with a sense of urgency. "I'm here, Mama!"

Come and see the beautiful field of flowers.

"But the field of flowers is turning red! There is so much pain! *I'm hurting!*" Tulip screamed, "Stop pulling my chest, it hurts! Something is hurting my Secret. Stop hurting me! I can't breathe! Too heavy! Please, please stop! Mama! Mama! Where are you?"

Tulip, Tulip, I am here, Sugar, the voice said.

"Mama! Mama! I'm coming to you!" Tulip yelled, overcome with pain from the violation of her body. She lost consciousness.

"Now that is the best piece of n—r ass I've ever had," Papa Betts declared aloud. "Even with all of that crazy n—r mumbo jumbo, it was still a pretty good piece of ass."

He raised himself off of the small, tiny figure under him. *Did I suffocate her?* he thought. He lifted his dirty boot and kicked at Tulip's buttocks and legs. Tulip moaned and tossed about like a slow-moving snake. Papa Betts was satisfied that she was alive because he had plans for her and he didn't want the law after him, even though the law didn't care much about another dead n—r.

Time to eat, he thought. He left the barn, leaving a raped, beaten, abused child to fend for herself in her pool of shame.

I can breathe now, Tulip thought, releasing a long, slow breath of air. She coughed as she took in the fresh air, but there was a burning in her throat. Tulip began to choke and coughed up blood.

No longer did she feel the heaviness on her chest, but she felt a burning sensation and pain vibrating through her small, young body. Blood trickled down her thin, brown thighs. The clean dress from the golden-haired lady was now torn, ripped, and cast away from her body. She lay naked and exposed.

Tulip lay in a fetal position. Every inch of her body ached with pain. She searched around the hay to find something to cover herself with. She tried to open her eyes, but she could only manage to open one. Through the one eye, Tulip looked around the barn in fear of this devil—surely, he was not human. She saw no one.

Tulip reached and pulled pieces of the discarded, ripped dress toward her. Even though the dress was torn and ripped, Tulip managed to cover her sore and abused body. Bite marks covered her small breasts, and clumps of hair had been discarded around her. Welts covered her thighs, and fresh, bright red blood poured from between her legs. She felt a swollen eye and lip, and blood ran from her nose and mouth. Tulip lay down on the straw and began to see the fields of flowers. Slowly, she drifted off into a deep sleep.

This is so strange. As my body drifts through the awful sea of pain
The field of flowers surrounds me, and
I seem to be a picture stuck in an unfinished frame.
No fear of feeling, no giving; it is like I have come and gone, yet not
lived long enough to know why I have come;
Either here or there, the reality escapes.
Could it be that life and dreams are one of the same...

Birds sang a song of spring to come. Many days came and went for Tulip at the Betts Farm—maybe even months or years, or so she thought. How could she measure time, when her life was being lived outside of her soul? Papa Betts was her master, her tormentor, her sin and shame, and her gatekeeper. The clean dress given to her by Mama Betts was now nothing more than dirty rags that she kept tied together about her violated body. Bugs infested her hair. Open sores covered her body. She smelled of vomit, blood, feces, urine, and some sticky, yellow emission that Papa Betts left all over her, especially in her mouth. The Betts children and Mama Betts were forbidden to speak with or go near Tulip. Papa Betts was her warden, and breaking his rules would bring about harsh punishment.

"Tulip, Tulip, wake up!" The golden-haired lady with the bluest kind eyes pleaded with a frantic softness. "Please, please, child, wake up," she said, gently shaking Tulip. Mama Betts could see that Tulip was in very bad shape. Looking upon the cuts, bite marks, and bruises on Tulip's face and chest and the dried blood that covered her small, brown legs, tears formed in Mama Betts's blue eyes and crept down her cheeks. *What a mean, good-for-nothing excuse of a man Papa Betts has become,* she thought, *to do such a God-unforgiving act to a child, no matter if she is colored.* Mama Betts refused to have the word n—r form upon her lips. She prayed.

"God, please have mercy of this poor, motherless child and forgive my husband, for he is a lost soul and is doing the deeds of the devil. I pray that you show mercy." She hated Papa Betts for these sinful acts.

Tulip had to wake up before he returned.

"Child, please wake up" Mama Betts called.

Tulip began to stir. "Mama, Mama," she whispered. Tulip slowly struggled to open her eyes. She could see a face before her, but she couldn't recognize it. The face was familiar, but unfamiliar. Tulip closed her eyes, but the face called out to her again. Everything was hazy, and it was dark and cold. Tulip was scared, and she wanted to go back to sleep.

Tulip looked around the room. Reality settled in as the inside of the barn came into view. She leapt away from Mama Betts, causing the older woman to lose her balance and fall backwards.

Tulip didn't take her eyes off Mama Betts. She wondered, *Did I hurt her?* Tulip didn't mean to hurt Mama Betts. The lady with the golden hair and blue eyes had been kind to her, but Tulip was scared. Mama Betts, shaken a little from the fall, managed to get to her knees and move closer to Tulip. "Don't be frightened," Mama Betts said lovingly. "I'm not going to hurt you, but I am here to help you. You've got to get up now and get to going before Mr. Betts wakes up," she said urgently, forcefully whispering to Tulip. "Do you understand me, child?"

Too afraid to answer, Tulip could only look down to the ground and slowly nod her head. Tulip wanted to reach out to the golden-haired lady and lay her head in the lady's lap for comfort, but she was too afraid to move or talk. Tulip wanted her Mama. Tears rolled down her face.

"Tulip, Tulip," Mama Betts repeated. "I know that you're hurting, child, and I know you're tired, but you've got to get going, you hear me? I can't help you. Mr. Betts is my husband, and I have to watch out for my own children," Mama Betts urged, almost apologizing.

"Now, I've a prepared a few scraps for you. This is all I can give. We have very little," she said with embarrassment. Mama Betts laid the bundle on the ground close to Tulip.

"Now, child," Mama Betts whispered to Tulip, "Pick up the bundle and be on your way as quick as possible, do you hear?"

Tulip stared in silence.

"Mister Betts is not a mean man and he doesn't mean to hurt you. Do you understand?" Mama Betts asked.

Again, Tulip's head hung down and she nodded in response.

As Mama Betts collected herself, she looked at Tulip with great sorrow and pity. She was truly a sad sight to behold. *A little colored, motherless girl child all alone out here among these men. What will become of her?* Mama Betts thought to herself. The mere thought brought a sudden chill, and she wrapped her homemade shawl around her body for warmth. *I will pray to God for her safe passage.*

With that, and with no further glance toward Tulip, Mama Betts departed from the barn.

Tulip took a deep breath. She felt faint, and began to throw up. Her empty stomach groaned from the lack of food. Her body ached from the violations and unprovoked beatings. Her soul cried for something familiar.

Tulip's mind began to recall the horror her body had suffered under the cruelty of her master. She questioned, *Why did he hurt my body? Why did he use his man parts to hurt me, my mouth, my Secret, even my backside, like an animal?* The man was vile and unnatural. *Why had he been so cruel? Why?"*

Tulip opened her legs and gently tried to clean herself with her ragged dress. The slightest touch of the dirty rag upon her Secret sent pain shooting through her body, causing her to bend over and scream. Tulip lay on the cold dirt floor of the old barn and cried. There were no more fields of flowers. No beautiful blue sky. No Mama. Just pain, blood, and hurt.

As Tulip lay on the floor, curled up like a newborn baby, the words of the golden-haired lady came rushing back to her.

Pick up the bundle and be on your way."

Tulip sobbed in fear and pain closed her eyes. She fell into a deep, hard, no-field-of-flowers sleep.

Tulip felt a hard, sharp kick to her head, then another kick to her back. Pain shot through her body. She cried out.

"Get up you filthy, lazy n—r!" yelled Master Betts. "See, looky here," he jeered. "My own n—r slave," he continued proudly, speaking to his friend Big Joshua. "I told you. Go ahead, touch her, she won't bite."

Since slavery was outlawed, Big Joshua knew that Papa Betts couldn't own this girl, but he could make her pay off her debt for eating his food and staying on his property.

"She's my very own n—r worker. I own her until she pays off her debt, and she is mine. I'm a wealthy man." Papa Betts stated with pride.

Big Joshua declared, "She ain't nothing but a little n—r child!"

"So, what's the difference?" Papa Betts yelled. "A n—r is a n—r, no matter what age. A n—r girl is meant for one thing only, and that is serving in whatever manner I see fit.

"Guess what, Big Joshua, my friend?" roared Papa Betts. "She got a tight little p—y, that will make you think you had gone to heaven."

Both men laughed. "She is a looker, even if a little young," Big Joshua mumbled, and greedily looked at poor Tulip, who was shaking in fear.

Tulip kept her head down while Papa Betts and his friend Big Joshua talked about her. Her heart was beating so loudly that she couldn't really hear what they were saying. That man, the master, was the one that had hurt her, and even now her head pounded from the kick he had just given her. The pain was constant, burning and aching. The bleeding had finally stopped, but now this man and the other one whom he called Big Joshua were staring at her with eyes that would scare the devil.

"So, what is it going cost me?" Big Joshua asked as he began to unhook the rope from his dirty, worn-out overalls.

"Since you're my best friend," Papa Betts began, "I'm only going to charge you two dollars. That's fair."

"Two dollars!" shouted Big Joshua. "You know that I don't have any money!" He yelled incredulously as he kicked the dirt and looked lustfully at Tulip.

"Would it cost anything for me to pee on her?" asked Big Joshua, with a big grin on his face. He had always wanted to pee on a girl. He was aroused from the mere thought.

"Pee? Did you say pee on her?" laughed Papa Betts. "Doesn't cost a man anything to pee," Papa Betts mused aloud. "Well, my friend, I guess you got a deal. Call it a free sample. *Ha*! In fact, let's pee on her together."

Big Joshua was overjoyed. He quickly unsnapped his pants and fully exposed his pointy, wrinkled, smelly penis directly in front of Tulip's face.

Tulip looked up in terror. Where could she run? Sweat began to form on her head while a small tear slowly trickled down her face. In the far distance she heard a dog bark. Someone called her name, and she smelled the field of flowers.

The potent urine from both Papa Betts and Big Joshua began to saturate Tulip's bruised body. It filled her nostrils, and Tulip gasped for air as if she was drowning, but she lay completely still, frozen in time, as she heard a sweet voice calling her name. *Tulip! Tulip! Come, Sugar, smell the flowers, honey, my sweet child.*

Mercy, she asked, show him mercy,
for he does not know what he has done;
The deeds of life will be judged by one's actions; we will be held
accountable for our actions;
We are our neighbors' keepers; take heed, because your death will
hail you as a savior or slaughterer!

chapter seven

Cuffed and Chained

"*I*s she dead?" asked the youngest Betts child. "She's really stinky." He then kicked her with his dirty, bare feet. Tulip did not move. "Why won't she wake up?"

"She isn't dead, and shut your stupid mouth before Papa hears us," said John Jr.

He knew that Papa would skin them alive if he found them with the n—r girl. Papa had made it very clear that they were not supposed to go near the barn where the n—r girl was. If they did not obey his words, they would be rewarded with a good whooping, and the Betts children knew that their Papa was true to his words. But, being the curious children that they were, they wanted to see the n—r girl.

John Jr. thought to himself what Papa had said about n—rs. *Papa said that n—rs were no better than dirt or s—t and should be fed to the pigs, but Papa spent a lot time in the barn with this n—r girl. Papa said that n—rs were not like whites. In fact, they were not better than dogs. God put n—rs on this earth to serve the white man and to lick the ground we white people walked on. Papa said that the color of n—r skin was proof that they were not favored by God.*

John Jr. looked at Tulip and he felt conflicted about the things that his Papa had said about n—rs. It was confusing to him because Mama never said the things that Papa said, but she didn't disagree with Papa, either. Mama just said that we were all human beings and the same, and that we were all God's children.

Did this include n—rs? And, more importantly, this n—r girl? John Jr. wondered. All this thinking made his head hurt.

"Ow! Ow! Mama, Mama," Tulip moaned. The two Betts boys were startled by the sounds coming from the n—r girl.

"She ain't dead!" the youngest Betts child yelled.

"Shut up, boy," ordered John Jr. "Didn't I tell you to be quiet? Do you want Papa to catch us?"

The boy kept his voice down. Tulip tried to move, but every bone in her young body hurt. She was aware that someone was with her, but everything was fuzzy. Were Master and Big Joshua still there? She was gripped with fear. Her mind was racing. She tried to focus on the two figures in front of her, wondering what pain they would wreak upon her. As her eyes began to focus, however, she saw that they were children, like her.

No, not like her. They were white children.

"She's looking at us," said the youngest Betts boy to his brother.

"I see her" stated John Jr. Not knowing what else to do, he spat on Tulip. Tulip continued to stare at him, so he kicked her leg, but not hard enough to hurt her. Tulip didn't cry out, and kept staring at John Jr.

Following his brother, the youngest Betts boy kicked Tulip with his dirty, shoeless feet. He tried to spit on Tulip, but only a few little drops came out of his mouth. Tulip continued to look upon John Jr.

The youngest Betts boy tugged at John Jr.'s ragged shirt. Annoyed, John Jr. yelled at him, with an impatient "*What?*"

The sudden, loud noise scared Tulip. She began to cry until she was sobbing uncontrollably. She kicked her chained legs, and her hands swung wildly above her matted, soiled hair.

Tulip began to feel rage holed up within her lungs. She didn't recognize the feeling, but it began to build as she looked upon John Jr.

Hands touching, grabbing, reaching, tearing, provoking, ripping. Pain, violation, humiliation; innocence lost, never to be regained.

chapter eight

The Great Escape

*M*ama Betts prayed as she pounded the dough to make biscuits for supper. She prayed to God to give her strength. She knew that her husband, the father of her children, was raping and beating the colored girl. It wasn't right. The girl wasn't his property. She belonged to *God*. Her husband wasn't a bad man. He was just a poor, unhappy man who had lost his faith in *God*. This little colored girl seemed to have brought out the devil in him.

Kneading the bread harder, Mama Betts's mind continued to race. *She is just a poor child, without a mother to love her—well, a colored child, but still a helpless, innocent child that God put on this earth. How can I teach my children God's love, when right before their eyes they see their Papa violating God's laws?*

My husband is not a mean man, only a poor man, she reasoned.

After Misses Betts's family perished in the fire, she was alone, afraid and confused. Many times, she questioned God. *How could you take my whole family? Why? Take me!*

When John Betts asked Karen to marry him, even though she didn't love him, she was relieved that someone wanted to watch over her. John Betts stepped up and helped with the burial of her family. He even spent his own money on some of the arrangements. At the time, Karen felt a lot of gratitude. She knew that John Betts was much older and had a decent farm. *It wouldn't be so bad*, she had thought. Besides, she didn't have many choices.

After marrying John Betts, she moved to the Betts Farm, about forty-five miles outside of Canton, New York. The farm was in disarray. The barn housed a few farm animals, including some horses, and several chickens, dogs, and kittens that ran about. There were acres of corn fields, as well as a small patch of other vegetables. The main house had a large wraparound porch. It needed a fresh coat of paint, and showed other signs of decay, such as broken windows and missing planks of wood. The front door had no knob or lock, and the wood was peeling.

Mama Betts remembered stepping inside an open, dusty, and dirty room and looking at what was going to be her home. Tears slowly escaped her blue eyes and rolled down her pretty white dimpled face.

Times were very hard, and the five children came fast. Life with Papa Betts was not easy. He hated being poor and longed for the riches his father had. Being poor made Papa Betts resent others who had more than him, especially the colored.

Mama Betts was distraught. Now Papa Betts had locked up this poor, motherless colored child. What could she do to make her husband see that hurting the child was wrong? *It is not God's way*, she pondered.

Then, she heard a scream emanate from the old dirty barn.

Mama Betts ran as quickly as she could. Was the child dying? Papa Betts had left earlier, and the children knew not to go into the barn, even if they heard the poor colored child's screams. But this scream was like that of a tormented animal. Mama Betts ran, clutching her chest, where her heart raced and pounded. Her breath was labored. "Please, Lord," Mama Betts prayed aloud, "don't let this poor motherless child be dying! Save her, Lord!"

Mama Betts swung open the barn door with such force that her children all jumped in fright.

"What is going on in here?" Mama Betts demanded in a loud voice. She saw Tulip lying in her own waste. The child's arms and legs were swinging wildly has she cried and mourned. Papa Betts had forbidden Mama Betts and the children from entering the barn, and she had not been there in weeks. Seeing Tulip in such dire conditions made her skin crawl and her heart break.

Mama Betts addressed the oldest son, "John Jr."

"Yes, Mama?" John Jr. softly replied, with down cast eyes.

"Didn't Papa tell you and your brothers and sisters not to enter this barn under any circumstances?" she asked, slowly.

"Yes, Mama," John Jr. barely whispered.

"Do you know what would happen to you and your brothers and sisters if Papa caught you in here?"

"Yes, Mama," John Jr. softly answered with tears streaming down his face. He knew what he, his siblings, and even their Mama would suffer if Papa Betts knew that they had disobeyed him.

"Mama," John Jr. said, "we just wanted to have a look at her. We didn't mean any harm."

"A look?" Mama Betts said, with heartfelt passion. "What do you think this poor colored child is? A freak at the state farm?" She looked upon each of her children with shame.

Tulip had stopped her screaming and thrashing upon hearing the voice of the golden-haired woman with the bluest eyes. A sort of comfort had taken over her as she listened to the woman speak.

"Now, John Jr.," Mama Betts continued, addressing her children and trying to manage her rage. "Take the children into the house. Get the Bible and hold it until I come in. Now!"

With that, each of the children ran from the barn, kicking a high cloud of dust from the barn's dirt floor.

Mama Betts slowly approached Tulip. "Hush, child, I won't hurt you. Nobody is going to hurt you anymore."

Tulip slowly lifted her bloodstained eyes toward the golden-haired lady. No words could escape her mouth. For the first time in weeks, however, she felt no fear.

Mama Betts helped Tulip sit up. The smell emanating from Tulip was horrible, worse than Mama Betts could describe. Mama Betts felt lightheaded, but she swallowed hard and drew her attention back toward Tulip. "Come, girl. Let's get you more comfortable."

She looked at the long chain on Tulip's raw, swollen ankle. Pus oozed from the cuts. Dried blood covered Tulip's battered body. Feces and urine surrounded her. The once-clean dress Mama Betts had given Tulip was now just torn, dirty rags that Tulip used in a pitiful attempt to cover her nakedness. Mama Betts noticed that one of Tulip's nipples had been bitten off. The sight made her gag.

With Mama Betts's assistance, Tulip sat up and leaned against the haystacks.

"You wait here," Mama Betts said, and headed toward the barn door.

Tulip didn't want the golden-haired lady to leave her like the field of flowers did. She wanted to scream, *Please don't leave me*, but her voice had no sound. Once again, tears stained Tulip's dirty, bruised, and bloody face.

As Mama Betts dashed breathlessly around the run-down farmyard toward the main house, she felt like a wild, crazed animal. But she knew she had little time before Papa Betts would return.

Inside the house, Mama Betts's quick and frantic movements startled the Betts children. They jumped to their feet, with eyes wide open. John Jr. was holding the Bible.

"John Jr.!" Mama Betts yelled, "Get the basin and fill it with hot water, and make no waste. Girls, go get one of your clean dresses."

"But Mama," they protested, "we only have one each for school and church. Which one do you want, Mama?"

"I don't care. You choose, and be quick!" Mama Betts frantically yelled in their direction.

Mama Betts moved quickly, tossing items into her apron pockets: soap, cloth for bandages, and salve for wounds. She stopped to catch her breath. Her heart was racing. Mama Betts knew that Papa Betts could be home in any minute, and there was no time to waste. No time to calm her pounding heart. She felt faint, and sweat rolled from her golden hair down over her pretty, weather-beaten face. She grabbed a jar of preserves, a hunk of bread, a few apples, and some carrots.

Mama Betts ran toward the barn, with the children following close behind. The two younger boys watched their Mama move frantically around the barn.

John Jr. loved his Mama and did not want to disrespect her, but he feared his Papa more.

"John Jr., I want to you leave the barn while your sisters and I help this child get cleaned up," Mama Betts said. "Doesn't the Bible say that we should help the weak? Well, this here is a child of God and we must follow God's command. I know that you do not want to disobey Papa, but God comes first, so please leave, so that I can do God's work."

John Jr. looked at his Mama with fear and tears in his eyes. He looked at the n—r girl with her head hanging low, making a whimpering sound like a hurt puppy. She was a pitiful sight. A little sorrow and shame entered his heart. He knew that his Mama spoke the truth, and that she would never lie. He looked at his sisters, whose heads were hung. With that, he placed the water-filled basin down near his Mama, gently touched her golden hair, and turned and left the barn.

After watching John Jr. slowly leave, walking like a man sentenced to death, Mama Betts turned her attention back to the poor child, who stood before her like death.

"Girls!" Mama Betts yelled, "Come help me."

The sisters could not take their eyes off of Tulip. Surely, this could not be the same little colored girl that came here only a few weeks ago. She looked like a monster, and the sisters were afraid. Also, Papa had told them not to come in the barn or go near her.

"*Girls!*" Mama Betts screamed, "Stop wasting time and come help me!" Mama Betts knew that her children were afraid of their Papa, but she had to get this colored child away before Papa Betts returned.

John Jr. slowly closed the old barn door, and tears rolled down his dirty red cheeks. John Jr. was a good boy, with good looks like his Papa once had. Despite being only twelve years old, he stood almost six feet tall. He had a head full of curly black hair and big brown eyes that were draped with long, black lashes. Big dimples creased both of his cheeks when he smiled, which he did often. His nose was straight and regal, like his Papa. He was as skinny as a pole, and had a big heart.

What to do now? John Jr. thought to himself. *Papa is surely going to kill me and Mama, or beat us half to death.* With his hands stuck deep into his pockets, John Jr. kicked at the dirt.

Suddenly, he heard horses. His heart raced with fear, and beads of sweat formed around his face. He watched as a horse and buggy slowly made its way up the long dirt path. "This can't be Papa," he said aloud. He ran as fast he could toward the barn.

Mama Betts turned her attention away from the sisters and looked kindly at Tulip, who stood motionless, with her head and eyes downcast. As she approached Tulip, Mama Betts began to speak in a slow and whispered tone.

"Now Tulip—that's right, your name is Tulip. Tulip, I am not going to hurt you, but I need to tend your wounds. Here, look: I have a little food, but first I need to clean you and get you dressed."

Tulip stood motionless, showing no signs that she understood what the golden-haired lady was saying.

Mama Betts reached out to touch Tulip, but Tulip shrieked in fear.

"Child," Mama Betts said lovingly, "As God is my witness, I will not harm you. See, it's just a little water and clean clothes."

Tulip slowly raised her head and tried to open her swollen, bloodied eyes. Kneeling before her was the golden-haired lady with outstretched hands. Tulip was confused and fearful. Had it been a dream that the golden-haired lady was kind to her before? Should she trust her? Tulip's head hurt, and things were unfocused.

Tulip could no longer stand. She felt herself falling, and collapsed into Mama Betts's arms. Upon seeing this, the sisters held each other in fear.

"Come, girls. Now." Mama Betts motioned toward the girls.

The oldest sister with golden hair and blue eyes like her Mama released her youngest sister and slowly approached her Mama. The youngest sister looked on with fear. The oldest sister kneeled beside her Mama and looked at the badly bruised body of the little colored girl. *Surely*, she thought to herself, *Papa did not do this to her, even though she was a n—r.*

"Here," Mama Betts said to her oldest daughter. "Take the rag and soak it in the basin of water."

As Tulip lay lifeless in Mama Betts's arms, Mama Betts slowly and gently began to peel away the torn and tattered rags from Tulip's battered and abused body. Some of the rags were stuck to the wounds, causing Tulip to whimper.

Together, Mama Betts and her daughters washed and tended to Tulip's beaten body. Tears slowly poured from their eyes as they treated her wounds. Seeing Tulip naked shocked Mama Betts. *What animal would do such things to a child?* Mama Betts thought of her husband. She had tried to love him. Early in their marriage, he had been a decent, hard-working man, but year after year, she saw how bitter he became because they were poor. Now, seeing what he had done to this defenseless child of God, Mama Betts considered her husband with detestation. She would never forgive him for these unfathomable acts and would pray for his soul. For now, he was with the devil.

Suddenly, the old barn door flew open. "He's coming!" John Jr. yelled. "Papa is coming!"

Mama Betts had just finished dressing and tending to Tulip's wounds, and was giving her water and food.

"Girls," Mama Betts called, "you stay put and don't come out of the barn."

Mama Betts slowly rose and wiped her hands on her apron as if she was preparing for battle. "God," Mama Betts prayed, "send your angels down to protect this motherless child and let no harm come to me and my children."

Mama Betts slowly walked to the old barn door. As she walked out of the barn, John Jr. followed his Mama closely. The two youngest children ran to their Mama upon seeing her. She patted them on the head.

As Mama Betts hurriedly walked out of the decrepit barn, her eyes squinted to get a clear view of the horse and buggy coming down the path. She put her hands to her chest. Her heart was pounding hard, as if she was running a race.

John Jr. walked up beside his Mama and reached over to take her hand, only to find that it was cold. He shook with fear. Together, they stood and watched the horse and buggy get closer.

"Hey there!" someone yelled from the buggy.

Like a gift from heaven, Mama Betts realized that the speaker was not Papa Betts. She and John Jr. looked at each other and smiled in relief. The youngest children played near their Mama's feet.

"Hey there!" Mama Betts called back. It was Luther.

From time to time, an old colored man named Luther would stop by to peddle some of the goods he picked up in his travels. Mama Betts didn't quite know where Old Luther lived, or how old he was. Old Luther was a fit, elderly colored man with smooth black skin, white hair, twinkling gray eyes and just a few yellow-stained teeth. He was a small-built, short man who stood no more than five feet tall. He was always polite, honest, and kind.

"Morning, Ma'am," Luther said, bowing his head and tipping his hat. "Just stopped by to see if your husband would like to look at some of these tools and goods that I have here for trade or to buy."

Mama Betts wiped her hands nervously on her apron. "Well, old Luther, my friend, you are certainly a sight for sore eyes!" she said, a little too loudly.

"Well, it's good to see you and your family, Misses Betts."

Luther liked Misses Betts. She was always nice and kind to him, and he preferred doing his business with her. Mister Betts always tried to cheat him because he was a Negro. In Luther's opinion, however, if he sold something that he came upon for free, then any price he received was a profit, and he never really felt cheated.

Mama Betts's mind raced. *This is truly a sign from God.* "John Jr., go to the barn, get your sisters, and take them into the house."

"But Mama," John Jr. protested.

"Go!" she insisted. Old Luther looked on, a little confused. He knew that John Jr. was his Papa's eyes and ears when Mister Betts wasn't around.

"Go now! I have business to conduct with Luther."

John Jr. stomped off, concerned for his Mama, and not wanting to enter the barn. "Sisters!" he called. They came running out with questioning looks about their faces. "Come on in the house!"

They were relieved to be out of the barn. The colored girl had just stared at them the entire time. The sisters dashed into the main house. With Old Luther and Mama Betts looking on, John Jr. gathered the young children and went into the house.

"Well," Mama Betts said smiling at Old Luther while nervously wiping her hands on her apron. "Now that that's done, Luther, please come down from your wagon and follow me. Quickly, please."

"Excuse me, ma'am," said Luther, taken aback by her request. He didn't want any trouble from her crazy, racist husband.

"Just come with me to the barn. I have something I want to show you."

At Misses Betts's request, Luther reluctantly followed her into the barn. As they entered, Misses Betts closed the door and told Luther to follow her.

"There," she said, as she pointed in the direction of the huddled, shivering, lifeless figure.

"What in God's name—" proclaimed Luther, upon seeing abused little Tulip with her knees pulled tightly to her chest and her head buried between her bruised, bloody legs. To Luther, it looked as if she and Death had crossed paths, and Death was close to being the winner.

Luther looked at her matted hair, blackened eyes, busted lips, and bruised arms and hands, and noticed the rope locked around the child's lifeless body, like cattle.

"Lord Misses Betts," said Luther, "who is this Negro child? Who done hurt this child?"

"Luther, please, I beg you, take her with you. Please, please Luther, you must take her now!"

"Misses Betts, no disrespect, but this ain't Luther's business," he protested, with eyes wide, shaking his head. He began to back out of the barn.

Mama Betts grabbed Luther's arms. "If you leave her here, she will die."

For a full minute, Luther and Mama Betts stared at each other.

Sensing that someone else had entered the barn, Tulip raised her head and looked up to see an old Negro man. He reminded her of the men that would stop and sell her Mama fruit and meat. She wanted to tell him, but her voice had no sound.

"Okay, okay!" Luther said with apprehension. "I reckon so, but I don't want no trouble."

Together, Misses Betts and Luther lifted Tulip's limp, bruised, broken body and carried her out of the place of torture and pain.

So lift my spirit, carry me off to the angels that I was meant to be
with, for I am not to be forgotten. Only He has the key;
Life is now soaring, a bird taking me to places for my eyes to see,
and a new world in front of me;
Memories are now a distant past; today is here to for me to see. Can
it possibly be that I am free?

chapter nine

Such Strange Relations

*L*uther saw the shadowy figure of Mister Betts as he made his way down the long, dusty path of the Betts's farm. Not fully understanding what he had gotten himself into, Luther knew that he needed to make haste. He picked up speed with his horse and buggy, trying to be mindful of his unexpected new cargo. Mister Betts and the Betts's farm began to fade behind him.

Luther continued down the road at a speedy pace for a few miles before he heard a stir in the back of the buggy. *So she's alive*, he thought, relieved. He didn't want to be moving around the countryside with a little dead Negro girl. Luther hadn't really gotten a good look at the girl because Misses Betts had nearly pushed him off the farm. Along with the child, Misses Betts had provided some bread, fruit and meat, which made good rations for the long trip Luther had to make, and two pieces of silver. But what to do with the girl who looked like she needed some serious care and mothering?

Tulip felt that she was on the move. The rough, bumpy ride of buggy made her uncomfortable. Pain shot through her sore body and she felt lightheaded from hunger. The last thing she remembered was the golden-haired lady talking to her. No more fields of flowers, no Mama, just blackness. Her dress was clean, however, and some of her wounds had been cleaned. She needed to figure out where she was.

Tulip looked about the wagon and saw an assortment of odds and ends. There were farm tools, bundles of wood, leather ropes, buckets, dishes, blankets, and other things. Tulip carefully lifted her sore body to get a better look at who was driving the wagon. She saw a small colored man with bushy gray hair. He was talking to himself and making grunting sounds.

"So, you're up?" asked Luther.

Tulip didn't answer.

"Cat got your tongue?"

Still groggy and shaken, Tulip did not answer.

"So, little girly, where you from? Where's your Papa and Mama? You a little thing out here all alone. Who whipped you up like that? How old you be around?"

Still Tulip sat silently.

"Now, if we are going to get along," Luther pointedly stated, "You need give me some answers, given I done risk my life." A thought occurred to Luther: *Maybe this here child is deaf and dumb.*

"Are you deaf? Are you sick in the head?" *How can she answer if she is deaf and dumb? Now who's the dummy?*

"Well, take your time, little girly. We got a ways to go while I figure out what to do with you. Lord, Lord, when you think you seen it all." Luther shook his head and began to whistle.

Tulip sank down to the floor of the wagon, afraid to think or look. She asked God to take her to the field of flowers. There, Tulip found beautiful flowers in colors of pink, white, yellow, and red. She was happy running and skipping through the field of flowers, surrounded by beauty, smelling the sweet scent that filled her nostrils with each breath she took. There, she felt no fear or pain. Only peace and happiness.

Tulip! Tulip! Someone called from a far distance.

Mama, is that you? Tulip questioned, as she looked around the beautiful field of flowers. *Where are you? They hurt me, Mama. I'm scared, Mama. Mama! Mama!*

"Hey, Hey! What is all of that fussing back there, little girly?" Luther asked, as he brought the buggy to a stop. He jumped down and walked slowly to the back of the wagon where Tulip was lying, shaking his head as he walked.

"What in tarnation have I gotten myself into?" Luther asked himself out loud. "If it wasn't for that nice, pretty Misses Betts giving me two pieces of fine sliver, I would have never agreed to take this mess of a colored child. What was it Misses Betts called her? A flower name, Tulip."

He would get a good penny for that fine sliver. He smiled at his good fortune. *But what about this little colored child?* He wondered. *She look pretty sick, like she been through a rough time. Looks like someone really worked her over, poor thing. God bless her soul.* Luther wondered if what Misses Betts told him about how she came about was true. But why would she lie to him? Why was Misses Betts in such a hurry to get rid of her? Now what is he to do with her? *I'm too old for trouble*, Luther thought, shaking his head.

Startled by Luther's voice, Tulip jumped up, trembling. The sudden movement caused her body to wring with pain. She felt dizzy and faint. Her stomach growled from hunger, her lips were cracked and dry, and she thirsted for a drink. She remembered the golden-haired lady lifting her from the cold, dirty barn, and there was a man—not the mean, evil man who hurt her, but a colored man who helped the golden-haired lady.

Tulip could hear Luther getting closer and closer to her. She cowered as close to the floor of the buggy as possible. She thought if she got as small as possible, the man would not see her. She heard the man mumbling to himself but couldn't understand what he was saying.

Tulip heard the slow drag of Luther's feet as he approached her. He grunted, coughed, and swore. Thoughts raced through Tulip's mind. *Who is this person? Would he also do those terrible things to me? God, please help me*, she prayed.

Suddenly, he was there, looking down at her. Tulip wanted to scream, but she had no voice. Tulip's eyes, wide with fear, locked on Luther's gaze.

"So, you're up!" Luther snorted. "My, my, you are just a baby," said Luther. "Chile, where is your Mama and Papa?"

Tulip lowered her head and cast her eyes down. She seemed to have become accustomed to this stance.

Reckoning that the poor child was frightened, Luther spoke kindly. "Come chile, I'm not going to hurt you," Luther said.

"Are you hurt?" Luther asked as he stared at Tulip. "Surely, you must be hungry." He smiled.

Sensing that the old colored man was trying to help and submitting to her need for food, Tulip simply nodded.

"Well," Luther said, smacking his leg, "now we're getting somewhere." He moved quickly to the other side of buggy. Tulip who moved quickly out of his way so that no contact would be made. Luther unwrapped the parcel of bread and meat and pulled off some pieces. He grabbed a cup and proceeded toward the forested area on the side of the road.

Tulip looked up to see where the small, old colored man had disappeared. She looked at the pieces of meat and bread laying on the buggy floor, but she dared not touch them. Her mouth watered, and the smell of the food penetrated her nostrils.

Suddenly, Luther appeared from the woods, grinning his

toothless smile. "I found us some nice, cool water from the spring below," he beamed. "This is a nice place for us to make camp for tonight. We have a long road ahead of us—" he paused. "Well, maybe just me. Not quite sure what to do with you.

"Here, have a drink" he said, handing Tulip the rusty tin bowl.

Without hesitation, Tulip grabbed the bowl and gulped the cool, refreshing water. As she drank, the water ran down her chin, neck, and chest until finally, Luther grabbed the bowl. Tulip coughed as Luther gently released the bowl from her hands.

"Now, now, you're drinking too fast. You'll choke, chile." Luther looked directly into Tulip's big brown eyes. It was then that he really looked at Tulip, and what he saw before him brought tears to his old gray eyes. In his lifetime, he had seen that look so many times, from his Mama, sisters, and aunts, and even some of his brothers. Here before him was a little colored girl who had been badly mistreated, and Luther knew in his heart the other horrible, indecent things that the poor child had endured.

"Now chile, take your time. There's a whole river down there with more water than you could drink in a lifetime. No need to be greedy—there's more." Luther tenderly handed the rusty bowl back to Tulip.

Tulip took the bowl, slowly this time, and raised it to her mouth, letting the cold water ease in as she swallowed.

Luther smiled, "Now, that's much better. Drink as much you want." Luther walked over to the pieces of bread and meat and passed a handful to Tulip.

Tulip set the water bowl down on the buggy floor and took the morsels of bread and meat. "Thank you," she managed meekly.

"Well, you are mighty welcome," said Luther, pleased.

Despite her stomach grumbling and hurting from hunger, Tulip timidly held the food.

"Go 'head, chile, eat up before some wild animal takes it from you."

With that encouragement, and remembering what the old gray man said about eating too fast, Tulip took small pieces, alternating between the meat and bread. They sat quietly, eating—an old, gray colored man and a small, motherless, broken colored child.

So true it is to be in this life at this time and not before or after,
it begs the question why;
Wondering if this is real or just a dream that is a heartbreak away
from the reality of what is to be;
Does it really matter how this time in space came to be, or should
every minute be spent as if this is the only time there is?
Living is not yesterday, not tomorrow, not before, not after,
not could have been, not even what may be;
it is now, so it is time to fly.

chapter ten

Going Nowhere Fast

oom! Boom! Thunder roared and lighting bolted through the
dark, cloudless sky so brightly that the sky lit up as if on a
sunny, radiant day. The enormous, ancient oak trees with sagging
limbs swayed and bent from the heavy rains and wind. The howling
sounds of the wind were like those of a trapped, wounded animal.
The dirt roads became thick with mud, red clay, and debris from
broken tree limbs. Luther's frightened horse trudged forward as he
whipped the back of the tired beast.

"Move your ass, Joey!" Luther yelled at the poor horse, which
was struggling with its burden through the heavy rains and wind and
trudging through the thick mud of the dirt roads. The horse yelped
at the sound of the thunder and was spooked by the sudden flashes
of bright lightning.

"Move it, move your ass!" Luther continued to yell at the
struggling horse. Soaked from the downpour of the heavy rain,
Luther said in a husky voice, "Gotta find some shelter until this
storm passes. Been on the road for more than three weeks and still
haven't reached New York City. That child slowed me up with her
whining, crying, and God-knows-what. I hope she worth the trouble.
Food almost gone, extra weight slowing me down…should have
been in the city days ago. Now this damn storm!"

"*Move your black ass, Joey!*" Luther belted louder at the exhausted horse.

Boom! Again, the thunder cracked. The wind cried out like a newborn baby in need of its mother's breast.

Tulip was huddled under the piles of boxes and crates in the buggy. She covered her ears to deafen the loud and frightening sound of the wind and thunder. She jumped when the lightning lit the trees of the woods, their branches casting ghostly shadows. Her imagination was running wild. Tulip tried to keep her eyes shut, but every now and then she would open them to get a quick peek of her surroundings. The lightning summoned ghostly figures reminiscent of that mean Papa Betts. His dirty, yellow teeth and smiling face would flash before Tulip, causing her to jump in fear. She wanted to jump from the old wagon and run as fast as she could, but the fear of Papa Betts's lingering face paralyzed her.

"Mama! Mama, where are you?" Tulip cried out. "*Mama!* Mama, where are you?"

A stillness came upon Tulip. Everything was quiet, and Tulip found herself drifting through a field of beautiful flowers. The scent of the flowers was intoxicating. Tulip was engulfed with all types of flowers; they surrounded her in shades of pink, purple, blue, yellow, and white. So many beautiful flowers. Tulip felt no fear or pain as she skipped along, touching each flower, taking in the sweet scent. Birds flew above, chirping away in unison. *Surely, this must be heaven. I never want to leave this place,* she thought to herself.

Tulip, Tulip, someone whispered softly.

"Mama! Mama, is that you?" Tulip called out as she looked around. "*Mama! Mama!*" she screamed.

"*Stop all that yelling,* gal!" Luther's voice bellowed through the pouring rain and wailing winds. "This storm is bad enough without all your fuss. Now hush it down, you hear?"

In the distance, Luther saw another horse and buggy approaching at a high speed. He could see the clothes of the oncoming driver blowing in the wind. The approaching horse's hooves were hitting the dirt road with a plundering sound that made Luther pull back on his own horse's reins in fear. He knew the muddy dirt road was too narrow for both to pass at the same time, especially at the rate of speed that the approaching buggy was going. This had to be trouble.

Luther narrowed his eyes to get a better look at the oncoming buggy. He wiped the rain and anxious sweat from his face. He could now see the buggy more clearly, but it was too late. Without any warning, they collided.

The crash was hard and sudden. Horses neighed in pain and both wagons flew into the air and came crashing down onto the muddy, rain-soaked dirt road. Boxes, crates, wood, clothing, and occupants came flying out of the wagons. The frightened horses broke free from the wagons and ran into the rain-soaked wood, leaving their owners to fend for themselves. The wagons rolled until they collided with a grove of large old oak trees, bringing them to a halt. The impact of the oak trees and the strong force of the storm winds snapped the wagons like paper kites. The sound of breaking wood from the wagons reverberated throughout the darkened, rainy woods.

Luther moaned and slowly lifted his head. He was thankful that he had landed in a soft bunch of bushes, but he felt bruised and sore. He didn't want to move too quickly, cautious of broken bones. The ground was wet, hard and cold. The rain beating upon his face slowly brought him back to his senses. It was dark, and the wind was howling. Luther carefully opened his eyes, but the rain, or possibly blood, was blurring his vision. He tried in vain to look around, but it was dark and windy. Everything was moving in slow motion, and his body was pinned under a large, heavy tree limb.

Pain shot up his leg, and Luther knew that it was broken. Another heavy limb was on his chest. Luther tried hard to focus, but he didn't see any movement. Suddenly, he heard a very faint moan. "Who's there?" Luther struggled. "Gal? Gal, is that you? Are you hurt? Are you okay? Yell so I can find you. Say something, chile!"

Aching with pain, soaked from the pouring rain, and disoriented from the sudden collision, Tulip struggled to raise her head. It was pounding with pain. Something wet trickled down her face, blurring her vision. Tulip managed to get to her knees. She looked around to see debris everywhere. Where was the old man? Suddenly, she heard a faint voice coming from the woods.

"Mister!" Tulip tried to yell. Her voice was barely above a whisper. Summoning all of her strength, despite the pain, Tulip stood upright. With the hem of her muddy, torn dress, she wiped the blood from her face and eyes. She could then see a little better through the rain and wind and could focus on the location of the faint cry.

Through the pain, Luther yelled as loud as he could, "*Over here, over here! I can't move! Over here!*" Feeling faint, he laid his head down on the sodden ground. He knew that the end was near. It was actually somewhat peaceful, this acceptance of death. Laying with his eyes wide open and breathing heavily, Luther looked toward the heavens. No longer was there lightning, rain, and wind pounding his face. No longer was pain wreaking his body. Instead, Luther felt warmth engulf him, and a feeling of sheer love.

Home! Luther's spirit slowly left his body.

chapter eleven

The Beginning

Tulip struggled to stand through the pain. "Mister! Mister Man!" she yelled. "Where are you?" She strained to hear through the wind and thunder. Her eyes searched the dark, scary woods and their ghostly aura. The large trees bent from the heavy rain and wind, forming fearsome figures. Thunder boomed, followed by streaks of lightning that lit up the woods. Tulip's fear-filled heart pounded hard and fast. She jumped at the sound of the thunder, turning in every direction until she felt dizzy and faint. Blood trickled slowly down her face and into her eyes, blinding her.

Suddenly, she heard a faint cry again. "Over here, over here," a voice cried out softly.

Tulip turned to search the woods. "Where are you? *Mister Man, where are you?*" Tulip screamed.

"Over here, over here," the voice faintly called out.

With outreached hands, blood, pain, and gut-wrenching fear, Tulip began to walk toward the voice. "Mister Man, keep talking so I can find you," Tulip yelled through the harrowing wind and drenching rain. "I can't see you, Mister Man."

"Here, here, over here," the muffled voice replied.

Tulip continued to struggle her way toward the sound of the voice. The loud thunder and flashes of lightning frightened her, but still she continued to walk toward the voice. Every muscle in her body hurt, and blood now covered her face.

It seemed that since Mama passed, Tulip had only experienced pain and suffering. *Why?* Tulip thought to herself, as she fought her way through the thick brush and woods. Small animals scurried about the woods, some running across Tulip's feet, causing her to her jump in fright. "Dear God," she cried, "I'm only a child. Help me, Lord. Help me." Tulip prayed out loud. "Mama, I need you," she cried.

Without any warning, Tulip tumbled over, landing face-down in a pool of red clay mud. Out of fear, frustration and sheer exhaustion, she kicked, screamed, and cried. Through her own cries, Tulip heard the voice call out to her.

"Help me, please help."

"Who's there? Is that you, Mister Man?" Tulip found her way through the red mud.

"Please, help me. I am stuck under this tree branch."

Tulip again used the hem of her soiled dress to wipe some of the red clay mud from her face, her eyes stinging from the onslaught of rain, blood, and dirt. Slowly, a figure began to take shape before her eyes. The heavy rain and wind made her blink. Tulip forced her eyes to focus on the figure lying. It was not Mister Man.

"Thank you, thank you. My leg is trapped under this tree," said the voice. "Please help me move it. I got to find my Paw. He must be hurt. Please, help me," pleaded the unfamiliar voice. With a flash of lightning, Tulip could clearly see the figure before her. It was not Mister Man, but a muddy, bloody boy her own age. A Negro boy.

Tulip stood frozen for a few minutes, just staring at that the strange boy before her. She could see him more clearly with each flash of lightning. She was dazed, frightened, and unsure whether or not she should help. Mister Man was nowhere in sight.

The boy moaned slowly. "Please help me, I got to find my Paw."

Tulip saw that the boy's right leg was trapped under a large tree branch. The boy had no strength to move his leg nor the branch. The rain beat down harder and the whipping wind made harsh, ghastly sounds.

Tulip began to tug at the large tree limb that had trapped the boy. She pulled with all the strength she had, but the unrelenting rain made it hard for her to get a good grasp on the limbs. Tulip continued to pull with all her might. As she pulled, the frightened boy began to pull his leg out from under the tree. He yelled in pain, but he continued to pull on the trapped leg. Tulip was slipping on the wet, muddy ground.

As she pulled, the boy yelled at her. "Good, pull just a little more! Pull, I am almost free." The wind seemed to pick up speed and blew harder. The lightning lit up the woods. The force of the wind and rain and panic seemed to be taking Tulip's strength. She was exhausted, but she continued to pull at the tree's limbs.

The boy reached out a grab a large tree root and pulled with all his might as Tulip pulled away at the limb. Finally, the boy dragged his leg free and collapsed from exhaustion. Tulip had pulled so hard on the limbs, her hands were covered in blood from several small cuts. She laid back against the nearest tree and looked at the collapsed Negro boy as she struggled to keep her eyes open. Within minutes, they both drifted off to sleep.

As they slept, it seemed that the forest became a protector over the two wounded, lost orphans. The large trees hovered over them as a shield against the pouring rain. The wind swirled around in a slow, rocking motion. The lightning and thunder began to quiet. The forest was still as the two children slept. They had found each other.

I lay upon thee in a labor of love,
for I not know what is to come
as we reach toward the walks of life.
Could this be the path chosen for us, or
is this just time to be spent in the search for what will truly be?
Behind us is the past that has led us to each other.
Let's move forward together to see what tomorrow has for us,
because it is not you, nor I, it is now we!

chapter twelve

Malcolm

*M*alcolm heard the faint sounds of birds singing in the distance. He felt dazed and disoriented. He lay very still and opened his eyes. He wanted to leap to his feet and fight anything and anyone, but Paw had taught him to always take his time, and not move until he had a sense of his environment and could analyze all the facts.

So Malcolm lay very still. He had to collect his thoughts before he moved. As he moved, pain shot through his right leg, and the memory returned, vivid and clear: the storm, the horse racing out of control, the oncoming buggy, and the collision.

"Paw!" Malcolm screamed so loud that Tulip jumped straight to her feet, and had to gather her senses. She stared, and the boy stared back, like a standoff.

Malcolm tried to make sense of the dirty, poor, black thing standing in front of him. She was certainly a sight: ragged and soaked to the bones, with nappy hair and bleeding hands. *Paw? Where is Paw?* Malcolm's mind screamed as his eyes began to frantically dart around the thick, foggy, forest. *"Paw!"* He began to yell, his voice echoing through the dense woods. He tried to stand, but the pain shot through his leg so forcibly that he fell back.

On hands and knees, he looked at the dirty girl and yelled in her direction. "We have to find Paw! *Find him!*" Malcolm pleaded.

Tulip stood up, shocked. She didn't recall seeing another man, only poor Mister Man, who was now in heaven with her Mama. Now this boy, or man—whatever he was—wanted her to find his Paw. Tulip stood motionless.

Malcolm began to cry. "Please, girl," he pleaded, with tears glistening in his eyes. "Please find my Paw. He's probably hurt and needs help. Please, I can't move, you have to help him! Please, whoever you are, please," begged Malcolm.

Malcolm and his Paw had been traveling to start a new life. Malcolm's Maw had died while giving birth to his baby brother, who died, as well. Malcolm and his Paw were heartbroken. His Paw took to drinking and stopped working. Malcolm, only seventeen years old, was a tall boy for his age, already six feet tall. He had striking features, with a long, pointed nose, high cheekbones, full lips, and light brown eyes: his Maw used to say that they were golden.

He was a kind and gentle soul. He understood his Paw's sorrow because he was hurting, too. He stopped his schooling to do odd jobs at neighboring farms. What little money he earned, his Paw used for whiskey. Malcolm knew his Paw was sad, but they had to eat and keep a roof over their heads. Work was hard to come by, and sometimes he worked just for a little food.

Malcolm's family were sharecroppers, and had to work the land for their keep. When his Maw was alive, there were happy times. She was a small, fair-skinned woman with long, curly hair and light eyes. His Paw was a tall, strong black man, with very black eyes, kinky hair, and a large nose that would spread across his face when he smiled. His Maw and Paw were nice to each other and took very good care of Malcolm. Before his Maw passed, Malcolm was going to school and had reached the fourth grade. The teacher said that he was quick and a fast learner. Life was easy, and Malcolm was happy. His Maw had said that he was a prince, and that one day, he would find his princess and live happily thereafter. Malcolm loved his Maw and his life. But that all changed when Maw and the baby died.

With Malcolm's Paw grieving for his lost wife and baby boy, Malcolm now had to earn food and money for both his Paw and himself. Malcolm understood in time that without working their own land, they would be forced to move. Malcolm tried talking to Paw, but it was no use. Most of the time, Paw just drank and slept.

While working on a neighboring farm, Malcolm overheard some of the farm workers talking about opportunities in the North for black people. Many were planning to take their families and move up there for a better life. Malcolm thought that this could be a chance for him and Paw. Malcolm couldn't wait to get home to tell his Paw, and if he wouldn't listen, Malcolm was strong enough to drag him off, if it came to that.

It was on that fateful journey that Malcolm's life would take another direction. Malcolm and his Paw packed up what little belongings they had. Malcolm kept one small keepsake from his Maw: a small golden locket. It had no chain, so Malcolm tied it around his neck with a rope. Malcolm sensed that his Paw was ready to move on. After mounting his horse, Malcolm's Paw took a long look at the poor rundown house they called home, took a swig of whiskey, and pulled off.

Oh, what roads we travel in our life,
never knowing from one moment to
the next where we are heading.
Our destiny is pre-determined, but not shared.
We can only try to guide our directions and hope that we are taking

the right steps, without any fear.
Ups and downs, around and around, happy and sad,
in and out, that is what all about.
But, life will always move where it is intended,
and we foolishly think that we are in control of every bend in the
road...so we think, so we will soon know...

chapter thirteen

Wounded by Fate

ulip finally understood that the boy was in the wagon with his Paw when the tragic accident happened. Tulip knew that Mister Man, who had helped her, was now in heaven with Mama, but she hadn't had time to say a little prayer for him.

What was to become of her now? Everything had happened so fast: the rain, the wind, the thunder and lightning, and the buggy crushing and rolling over. She didn't even know there was another buggy until the boy screamed out to her for help.

Tulip had to help this poor boy. He looked big enough to be a man, but his face looked like that of a boy. When she looked into his pretty, light eyes, she felt dizzy. She was hungry, and her stomach rumbled for food. She was cold and wet from the rain. Her hands were torn and still bleeding from pulling on the tree limbs. *Where could his Paw be?* Tulip wondered.

"Okay," Tulip said to the hurt boy, while trying to wrap her mind around what was expected of her. "Let me look for your Paw." *What if the boy's Paw was hurt or had passed on, like Mister Man?* What was she to do? She was tired, hurt, hungry, wet, and confused herself. But the boy needed her, like Mama had needed her, so she would help. Mama expected her to help, and for some reason, she wanted to help this boy. Tulip knew what it felt like to lose your parents. In her short life, she had lost both.

Tulip told the boy that before she could look for his Paw he had to sit down, because he was hurt, and his leg was bleeding. She looked at the boy's leg and saw an open wound with raw flesh visible. The sight made her want to vomit, but there was nothing in her stomach to release. She didn't want to look at the wound, but she had to. Tulip wiped her bloody hands on her torn, dirty dress. She reached under her dress and tore a piece of cloth. The cloth was wet, but clean. Tulip explained to the boy that she needed to wrap his leg to protect it while she looked for his Paw.

The boy looked into Tulip's eyes, and though he did not trust her completely, he saw something that made him relaxed. Through the grime and dirt, he saw that Tulip was rather pretty, and kind. He felt something unusual, and though he was confused about his feelings, he had no strength or desire to resist her helping him once again.

Tulip carefully wrapped the boy's leg. He was quiet, but watched her very carefully. He tried to be still, but his leg was hurting, and he wanted to cry, but he didn't want this dirty girl to think he was baby. He needed a distraction from the pain.

"My Paw and I was heading North for a new start. We didn't know that a bad storm was coming—well, I sort of felt the rain in the air, but I didn't think it was going to be as bad," Malcolm continued, while avoiding eye contact with Tulip. "We had been traveling for a few days without much rest or food. We took turns driving the buggy. Our horse, Maggie, she was getting really tired. We probably were pushing her too hard. Paw was driving when the hard rain started up. It got dark and windy so fast. I guess Maggie was a little spooked by the heavy wind and thunder. Paw was going really fast. I guess trying to outrun the storm."

Tulip worked on his leg and listened, avoiding the boy's eyes. It felt funny to Tulip be so close to this boy and to be touching him.

Malcolm continued talking. "It got so dark and the tree limbs were whipping about our faces. The rain was blinding, and I knew it was hard for Paw to see on this narrow road. I just remember a loud sound and tumbling and rolling and crushing. I heard Maggie scream out in agony. Poor Maggie. She was the best horse ever. I don't know what happened to Paw, because I was thrown from the buggy." He turned to Tulip, clearly upset. "That's why we got to find him. I know that he's alive and hurt, and looking for me."

Tulip looked at him and nodded, without speaking.

Malcolm, getting more upset, looked at Tulip and asked rather forcibly, "*What's your name, girl?*"

While tending to Malcolm's leg, Tulip had listened to him and realized that she liked the sound of his voice. He had a strong, deep, kind voice. The words flowed clearly from his mouth, almost like a song. It was nice. But now, when asking her name, Malcolm seemed hard and demanding. Not liking his tone, Tulip slowly turned to look at him and stare into his eyes, without speaking a word.

This was unsettling to Malcolm. He never had a girl look so deeply at him. He had his way with a few girls, but none had ever really looked at him.

Malcolm looked at Tulip and gently said, "I didn't mean to be stern. It's just the pain and I am so worried about my Paw. I'm sorry." Malcolm lowered eyes, as if shamed by Tulip's stare.

Tulip was touched by his kindness. Since her Mama died, she hadn't experienced much kindness. Mister Man was kind and he had helped her, but now he was gone. Tulip decided that after she looked for the boy's Paw, she would say a prayer for Mister Man.

"Tulip is my name," Tulip said softly, without looking up.

"What's yours?"

"Malcolm," the boy replied. Agony hid behind his tightly shut eyelids. "My name is Malcolm."

Without warning, he fainted.

Oh, how the roses grow, like a splendor in the grass.
How sweet they are, like the first look and smile.
This is a strange feeling, like a fleeting past.
Something familiar, but not quite the same as an hourglass.
Time goes slow and you want it to last,
because this is new, exciting, and so sweet and tender.
Two paths have crossed, a life is forming, and who would have
guessed the hour and time that their hearts would be free?
So go loving, my two, your lives together will be joined forever in
whatever time that is meant to be.

chapter fourteen

Saying Goodbye

*A*fter she finished tending to Malcolm's legs, Tulip told Malcolm to stay put while she looked for his Paw and any sign of their horse Maggie. She feared that both horses had run off after the terrible accident. What if Malcolm's Paw was hurt? How could she help him? She was just a child. Worse, Malcolm's Paw could be dead, like Mister Man. *Poor Mister Man.*

As Tulip began to walk further into the woods, she began to feel afraid. It was strange looking at the tall, bent, hanging tree limbs with fog ascending from the ground. It was eerily quiet. Now and again, she heard a *yep* from some sort of animal. As Tulip walked farther, she felt so alone.

"Mama, Mama," Tulip said softly to herself, "Where are you? I don't smell the flowers. I'm scared, and I don't know what to do. Help me, Mama!"

Tulip heard a very soft whisper. *Just smell the flowers. Mama is here, just smell the flowers,* a voice said sweetly.

Suddenly, Tulip saw what appeared to be a buggy. She wasn't sure if it was Mister Man's or Malcolm and his Paw's buggy.

The boy has a name. Malcolm. She let out a little giggle. *No time to be silly*, she reasoned.

Tulip gingerly walked toward the overturned buggy which had

been smashed to pieces. All of its contents had been thrown about. There was a pile of blankets, a variety of salted meat, preserves, millet, honey, coffee, a big sack of flour, potatoes, a couple of pots, and some knives, cups, and spoons. Unfortunately, the dishes were broken into pieces. This didn't appear to be Mister Man's buggy.

Tulip moved closer to the buggy, and she jumped in fright. There was a hand sticking out from underneath. The hand was not moving. Tulip moved carefully around the buggy to get a better look.

She immediately jumped back. A long black snake was moving over the hand and up the arm. *Could this be Malcolm's Paw?* Tulip stood for what seemed to be hours, contemplating what to do. Tears slowly streamed down her face. Malcolm's Paw was now with Mama and Mister Man.

Tulip moved past the snakes. Mama had taught her how to move out of the reach of a snake. Her stomach cramped and growled from hunger. She pressed her sore hand against it to quiet the sound. She tried to pick up the buggy, but she had no luck. Tulip looked around and listened for any sounds of Malcolm's horse Maggie and Mister Man's horse Joey, but they were nowhere to be found.

With no horses in sight, Tulip began to look at the contents of the buggy strewn about the ground. Tulip picked up a potato and wiped off as much mud as she could and bit into it. The potato was hard, but it was good. As she ate, she looked for other items that she could use, but it was not possible to carry them.

Tulip saw a few blankets lying on the ground. While they were wet and muddy, she could use them to carry what she could salvage. Tulip proceeded to carefully bundle the millet, preserves, salted meat, pots, tools, and other items. *Good idea,* she thought, allowing herself a brief moment of satisfaction.

Tulip hurried to collect as much as she could. But the bundle was too heavy to move. Though she was loath to do so, she took out some of the contents to make the bundle easier to drag. Tulip slowly pulled the bundle as she walked back to Malcolm. She was trying to form the words to tell Malcolm that his Paw was gone. Even though she knew neither Malcolm nor his Paw, she still felt sorry for them. Tears flowed freely from her eyes as she walked back toward Malcolm.

As Tulip got closer to the spot where she had left Malcolm, she felt a stillness. *Maybe the boy has fallen asleep.* As she approached the spot, Tulip felt a tightness in her chest. There was no Malcolm in sight.

In a panic, Tulip released her hold on the bundle of goods and ran to the tree where she had left Malcolm. *How could he have moved? Did someone take him?* Tulip thought with dread. Tulip turned to her right, then her left.

"Where is he?" She said with fear. Forgetting his name, she yelled, "Boy, boy! Where did you go, boy? Boy! *Boy!*" Tulip screamed in fright. Suddenly, she heard a crushing sound, like leaves being stepped on. She turned around.

There stood Malcolm, grinning. "What you yelling for, girl?" he asked, smiling. "Where do you think can I go with a hurt leg and all? And who is 'Boy?' My name is Malcolm. In fact, my name is Malcolm Julius Thornton, Jr., named after my Paw."

Suddenly, Malcolm remembered that the girl had gone looking for his Paw. "My Paw, my Paw! Did you find him? Is he hurt? Tell me, where is he? Take me to him," he pleaded, with a serious look on his face.

Tulip could only stare at Malcolm, with silent tears streaming down her dirty face.

Malcolm began to panic. "Say something, girl!" he yelled.

"Don't just stand there. Did you find my Paw? Where is he? Take me to him, or else!"

Tulip just lowered her head and clenched her fists tightly. There were no words.

Becoming frustrated with Tulip's lack of response, Malcolm began to lean on the stick that he was using as a cane and struggled to walk in the direction from which Tulip had come.

Malcolm mumbled, as he slowly hopped along, "You can't expect a girl to do a man's job. I will find my own Paw, you stupid girl." But Malcolm was moving too quickly, and he tumbled to the ground.

"S—t," he cursed, not from the menacing pain, just from the need to find his Paw. The makeshift cane had broken apart. Malcolm began crawling on his hands and knees. Tears began to form in his eyes, streaming down his dirty face. The ground was hard and rough, cutting at his hands and knees, but he continued to crawl. Malcolm knew what the girl's silence meant, but he had to see for himself.

Tulip was overwhelmed with sorrow and pain, watching Malcolm trying to drag himself to his Paw. She knew what it was to lose family. She walked over to Malcolm.

"Let me help you," Tulip said softly.

Malcolm didn't want Tulip to see him crying, so he quickly turned his face away and shouted at her to leave him alone.

Tulip stood firm. She asked, "So what, are you going to drag your way through the woods? Your hands are already bleeding. Here, let me help you." With her head lower, Tulip added gently, "And I'll take you to your Paw."

Malcolm looked at Tulip for what seemed an eternity. Wind slowly caressed the trees, birds flew by, and no other sound was heard.

Tulip looked and Malcolm and said, "You can lean on me. I know that you're hurting, but we only have each other now." With that, Tulip reached down and pulled Malcolm to his feet. It was a struggle, but she managed.

Malcolm tried not to put too much weight on Tulip because she was just a little thing, but she was strong, and held his weight.

Slowly, they walked together, feeling a sense of closeness that they had not experienced in a long time. Malcolm did not want his mind to wander; his focus was on his Paw, but he was curious about this girl. They passed the large bundle of provisions that Tulip had abandoned when she thought that Malcolm had left her.

"That's my blanket," Malcolm said, looking puzzled. "How did it get here from the buggy?"

Tulip shyly replied, "I found these things laying in the woods, so I gathered them for us. I figured we would need them."

Malcolm had to ask. "So, Paw—" He couldn't finish, knowing the answer.

"Yes," said Tulip, as gently as possible. Together, they dragged along.

Malcolm was beginning to feel a little faint. He was hungry and the pain in his leg was increasing, but he couldn't stop until he found his Paw.

Suddenly, there it was: the overturned buggy. Malcolm wanted to run toward it, but he couldn't. "Paw! Paw! I'm here! Paw! Paw!" As they got closer to the buggy, Malcolm saw the outstretched hand. He pulled away from Tulip, fell to the ground, and crawled to his Paw, sobbing.

Tulip just looked on, feeling helpless. In that moment, she felt for the boy. "Mama," she called out softly. "Help this boy and let him smell the flowers." The forest was quiet. Nature and the animals grieved with Malcolm for his loss.

Time passed slowly. Malcolm managed to regain his composure and slowly dried his eyes. He knew he had to bury his Paw, but how? If Tulip could lift the buggy just a little, he could pull his Paw out from underneath.

"Girl—I mean, Tulip," Malcolm corrected.

Hearing her name, Tulip jumped. "Yes?"

"I need your help," said Malcolm, looking embarrassed because of all the emotion he had displayed in front of a stranger, let alone a girl. *She probably thinks I'm weak*, thought Malcolm.

Tulip quickly rushed over to him. "Help me to my knees," said Malcolm. "Please."

Tulip reached down and helped as asked. Malcolm reached under the buggy and grabbed his Paw's arm and began to pull. Tulip thought to herself, *What is he doing? There may be snakes under there.* But she kept her thoughts to herself because she would do the same if that was her Mama under that buggy.

"Can you help me pull my Paw from under this buggy?"

Tulip stood wide-eyed and transfixed. She knew Malcolm's Paw was gone and she didn't want to touch no dead person. She didn't touch Mister Man. She just covered him with some leaves.

"Tulip, help me," demanded Malcolm. It seemed as if the boisterous sound of his voice made the birds flutter. Malcolm announced, "I will not leave my Paw here like an animal. Now you move your little ass and get over here and help me. *Now!*" screamed Malcolm, feeling hurt and frustrated over his need for her help.

Sensing the rage in Malcolm's voice, Tulip moved quickly to his side. Together, they pulled with what little strength they had until Malcolm's Paw was finally freed from the buggy.

Upon seeing his Paw, Malcolm was overcome again with grief.

He held his Paw closely and rocked, while stroking his Paw's head.

Tulip sat nearby and watched with tears filling her eyes, remembering her Mama.

My, what a strange thing is this thing we call living.
One minute it's here,
and the next minute it's gone in the dust,
seamless or in the vast sea drifting;
It's glorious, wonderful, unexpected, loving, hard, and easy.
Life is living, feeling, and giving.
Living is life, just as dying is death.
Like the wind in time that moves slowing,
the grass grows green and brown within a day,
the sun rises and fades away,
like a favorite song you heard to which you sing along,
I want to be free, live, grow,
love, and play forever in a day.

chapter fifteen

To the Dearly Departed

he wind slowly blew the leaves on the trees. The leaves swayed back and forth on the limbs until they drifted slowly to the ground, as a feather floating in the air. The air was cooling as the sun began to fade from the sky. Night was coming, and Tulip and Malcolm had only just finished laying Malcolm's Paw in his roughly-made grave.

"I will mark this place, and one day, Paw, I will come back and give you a right and decent burial. But, for now, this must do," a sorrow-filled Malcolm promised.

Tulip looked on as Malcolm lowered his head in prayer.

Dear God, here lies my Paw, Malcolm Julius Thornton, Senior.
He was a good husband to my Maw and a good Paw to me.
He worked hard and did the best he could in this life.
He is now yours. I hope that you do right by him.
I'll see you again, Paw. Say 'Hello' to Maw up there in heaven.

Malcolm stood very still and stared down at the ground. Tulip also stood still, not wanting to disturb him. With darkness now engulfing them, hunger pangs gnawed at their stomachs and pain once again gained their attention.

Malcolm looked in Tulip's direction, like he was seeing her for first time. "It's dark now, so we better settle in for the night," he said.

"If you help me, we can turn the buggy upright and bed down for the night. I can make a fire to keep us warm while you gather some of the food for us."

Tulip nodded her head, but just stood still.

"Are you alright, girl?" asked Malcolm.

"Yes," Tulip replied quietly.

"Well, you need to get moving. Like I said before, it will be too dark to see soon."

Tulip sadly looked at Malcolm and said, "What about Mister Man?"

"Who is hell is Mister Man?" Malcolm asked, looking puzzled.

Tulip didn't know how to explain to Malcolm how Mister Man and Mama Betts had helped her to escape from Papa Betts. She would never tell Malcolm the terrible things that happened to her at the Betts Farm. It all seemed like a dream. Never, never would she tell anyone. What would she say?

"*Well?*" yelled Malcolm, making Tulip jump in fright. "Who in the damn hell is this Mister Man and where in the hell is he?"

Tulip's Mama taught her not to lie because it was a sin. But she couldn't tell him those awful things. Tulip felt the urge to pee. She had been holding it for a long time. "I got to pee!" she yelled.

"Pee?" smirked Malcolm. "First, we got to find this mystery Mister Man, now you got to pee. What's wrong with you, little girlie? Are you alright up there in your head? You not coo-coo, are you?"

Tulip just stared at Malcolm. Malcolm stared at her.

"Well, go ahead and pee, who stopping you?"

Tulip looked at him in shock. She would not pee in front of this boy with his staring eyes. Too many had already seen her Secret. No more. Tulip walked a little and went behind a big tree. Realizing that she was trying to relieve herself, Malcolm became embarrassed, and turned his back.

Taking the time to relieve herself also gave Tulip time to think about how she would explain herself to Malcolm. She asked God and Mama to forgive her for telling lies, but she had to take care of herself and create a new history for her life. Tulip took comfort in knowing that Mama and God would forgive her.

Peeing had become difficult because of the pain. She needed to bathe because she was beginning to smell herself. Moving from the shelter of the tree, Tulip stepped out slowly with her head down.

"Mister Man was my Papa," she said, looking down at the ground. It was getting dark. To her relief, it was hard to see Malcolm's face. Soon, they would need to start a fire, she thought.

"We were on our way to start a new life, like you and your Paw," Tulip continued. Closing her eyes made it easier to lie. Mama went home to be with God, which was not a lie, Tulip thought. "My Papa wanted us to start over again in a new place. He was sad after Mama died." Tulip kept her fingers crossed behind her back. She didn't want God to strike her down. Lying was hard and her stomach was hurting even more than before.

"My Papa and I were traveling to sell some goods so we can have money for our travels. We lost our house in a fire. That's how Mama died." This was partly true, thought Tulip. "Papa saved me from the fire, but I get confused sometimes, because I hit my head. That's why I call my Papa Mister Man, though I know he's Papa." With that, Tulip looked up at Malcolm.

"Well," Malcolm asked, "Is your Papa dead too?"

"Yes," said Tulip. "He was thrown from the wagon and I saw him bleeding from the mouth. I tried to help him but it was no use.

I was hurt and not strong enough, so I couldn't help him.

"Where is he?" asked Malcolm. "Don't you want to bury him?"

"I do, I do, but I didn't want to ask you because you just lost your Paw," said Tulip.

"I thank you for that," said Malcolm, "but respectfully, we need to bury your Paw. It's the decent and godly thing to do. You helped me with my leg and helped bury my Paw, so it's only right that I repay my debt." Malcolm continued, "It's too dark now, but first thing in the morning, you show me where he is. You don't want to leave your Paw in the woods for wild animals to eat."

Tulip hadn't thought of that. While she hadn't known Mister Man very long, he saved her from that mean Papa Betts. Plus, he was nice to her. She didn't want to leave Mister Man's body lying in the woods for God-knows-what. Malcolm was right, it was too dark now, and morning would be best.

Interrupting Tulip's thoughts, Malcolm stated, "It's getting colder and darker. We need to get moving with the buggy, but I am sorry for your loss."

Tulip looked at Malcolm, but could not reply. She moved to the buggy and motioned to him. The buggy was heavy, but even with Malcolm using only one hand, they managed to turn it upright. Underneath the buggy were more provisions.

Malcolm told Tulip that he would start a fire. Tulip found a blanket, but it, too was soaked and muddy, so there was nothing to protect them from the cold night, though the fire would help. Tulip found some potatoes, onions and carrots. There was no water to wash, so she found some clean clothing and started wiping off the dirt has best she could. She would also save some cloth for Malcolm's leg.

Malcolm roasted the vegetables as Tulip huddled close to the fire. He handed Tulip a hot, roasted potato on a stick. "Let it cool a little. You don't want to burn your tongue," he said with a little smile.

Tulip gave a little smile and took the stick with the roasted potato. Strange night sounds came from woods as wild animals scurried around. The wind blew gently. Tulip was thankful that the storm had passed, but was sorry for their losses.

Hearing a noise, Malcolm jumped up and put his hands to his lips, warning Tulip not to make a sound. The sound of crunching leaves was getting closer. Malcolm looked around for something to use as a weapon. He slowly picked up a big piece of wood and held it high. His eyes searched the dark woods as the crunching sound grew louder and louder.

To his amazement, it was old Maggie, his horse!

Malcolm ran to Maggie and hugged her with joy. "Look at you, old girl," Malcolm said to Maggie. "Tulip, hand me one of those potatoes and some carrots from the buggy."

Tulip got up and fetched the food and handed it to Malcolm.

Malcolm fed Maggie, who ate greedily. That's a good girl," Malcolm said, stroking her. "Old Paw is gone, so it's just you and me."

Tulip looked on and felt the love that Malcolm had for his horse. She missed Mama's love.

Malcolm felt a little better having Maggie back. It eased his pain of losing Paw. He sat down by the fire and returned to roasting the food. He looked at Tulip, who was watching him carefully.

"You can sleep in the buggy and I will stay here to watch over the fire. But we will need to get a move on early to bury your Paw."

Tulip nodded in agreement and felt the pain in her stomach.

Morning came with big, bright rays of sunlight streaming

through the trees. Tulip rose to see that Malcolm had placed the bundles on Maggie's back. Tulip's body ached the from the hard wagon ride and crash of the day before. She wished she could bathe.

"You up?" asked Malcolm. "There's some breakfast for you. While you were sleeping, I found a stream with fresh water."

Tulip wondered how he managed with that hurt leg.

Malcolm handed Tulip a hot cup of coffee he had just made. It was good and warm. Tulip drank the coffee and ate some dry meat that Malcolm had left for her.

"If you walk down a little, I left a bucket of water for you to wash."

Tulip was at a loss for words. *How did he do all of this?* she thought. "Thank you," was all she could manage to say while avoiding Malcolm's gaze.

Feeling cleaner and fuller, Tulip asked Malcolm if she could tend to his leg. Tulip had torn some clean rags from the clothing in the buggy. She used some of the fresh water to clean the wound. Malcolm gave her two boards from the buggy, one for each side of his leg, which Tulip tied tightly. With the support of the boards, Malcolm was able to move about with less pain. He thanked Tulip and said he was ready to find her Paw.

With Maggie loaded and the fire put out, Tulip began to walk in the direction where Mister Man was thrown from the buggy. It had been dark, but she was sure that she could find him.

After walking for about fifteen minutes, Tulip finally came upon Mister Man. Red ants were feasting upon his body. Tulip turned her head.

Sensing what he thought was her sorrow, Malcolm took a blanket from Maggie's back to cover Tulip's Paw. He felt sorry for her, because they had both lost a loved one.

"Come, Tulip," Malcolm said very gently. "We must bury your Paw."

Tulip turned to face Malcolm with tears flowing from her eyes. She was sorry for Mister Man and sad that he lost his life. She made a promise that she would find his loved ones and tell them where he was buried.

After they dug a crude grave, Malcolm saw that Tulip was having a rough time, and said a little prayer.

> *God bless Tulip's Paw because surely, he was a good man*
> *who was taking care of his daughter when he lost his life.*
> *May he find his wife in heaven and*
> *they can be together forever. Amen."*

Tulip just stared.

With the burial completed, Malcolm knew that he was now responsible for the strange little girl that he barely knew anything about. How could he take care of her? He hardly had the means to take of himself. *Maybe she has family somewhere, but where?* He wondered.

"Girl—I mean, Tulip, do you have family that we can find for you?" asked Malcolm.

"No," Tulip replied, "Papa was the last family I knew. I guess I have to make a way on my own."

Malcolm stood with his head hung low. He looked to the dirt ground for some answers, which would not come. "You saved my life and I am beholden to you. If you let me know what I can do to help you, I am willing to try," Malcolm said, looking up toward Tulip.

Tulip looked at Malcolm and realized what he was asking her. "I have no one. No more family other than maybe some distant relatives but I ain't never met them and don't know where to find them. Like you, my Papa was my only family. Lord took my Mama aways back," Tulip whispered, with tears misting her eyes.

Malcolm was at a loss. He couldn't leave this girl by herself, but he couldn't be responsible for her. He could barely take care of himself. He considered what to do. Maybe they could get to a town and he could find someone to take her in. She was strong and could work. She seemed to have good sense. She also wasn't bad to look at, even if she *was* just a child, and though he didn't know exactly how old she was, she was old enough to work. *Just until we get to a town,* Malcolm thought to himself. *Then I will have paid my debt to her.*

My, My, what little webs we weave
like a spider drawing in its prey;
the light is not bright for us to find our way,
but the dark gives us time to think and maybe,
just maybe, gives us time to play.
We know not what direction life is taking,
but we move forward, because there is no behind.
Each step we take is leading us to the place that is called our path.

chapter sixteen

Love by Another Name

*T*ulip and Malcolm moved along the roads without any way to gauge time or direction. Life seemed to start the day with the sun and birds chirping and end it with darkness and sounds of the wild. The roads were endless and no one else seemed to travel. Malcolm didn't know where they were. His travels with his Paw had been limited, visiting only nearby farms and local stores. He knew that days, even weeks had passed since he and Tulip had started on the road. While water was plentiful from many streams, food rations were getting low. Malcolm knew it was possible that there were farms within the depths of the forest, but he figured it was best to stay on the main road.

He wondered if he could do a little fishing or catch one of the wild animals in the forest. His hunting skills were limited, but he was sure he could figure it out. There were also plenty of wild berries and fruit trees. They wouldn't starve. But a nice, hot, home-cooked meal with some cornbread—or better, biscuits dripping with sweet apple butter and a hunk of salted ham sure would have been good. Just thinking about good food made Malcolm's stomach growl in protest.

Malcolm turned to Tulip and wondered if she was hungry and whether or not she dreamt of good vittles like he did. She never whined or complained like the other silly girls her age. In fact,

Malcolm found her to be very helpful. She worked just as hard as he did. He liked that she wasn't a chatterbox, constantly talking like some of the girls that attended his schoolhouse. They were always talking, laughing and sneaking peeps at him. In fact, Malcolm found Tulip to be rather quiet, and always deep in thought. She didn't seem to be sad but just looked like she was thinking to herself. Malcolm liked that Tulip kept herself clean as best as she could, considering the circumstances.

Tulip made sure Malcolm didn't see her naked, and stayed far away when she bathed in the streams. Sometimes, she would jump when he made a sudden move toward her. Like a frightened little puppy, her eyes would go wild. Malcolm could sense she had a lot to her story, even at such a young age.

Malcolm looked at Tulip very slyly. He was careful not to stare. She had beautiful brown skin and very pretty light brown eyes. They were almost transparent. In fact, Malcolm thought that, with the exception of his Mama, Tulip may have been the prettiest girl he knew, even though he admittedly didn't know that many. Once she fixed her hair and put on some nice, clean clothes, she could be beautiful. One day, she would make a man a fine wife, and have a bunch of children. Malcolm wondered if she had ever been that way with a boy. He blushed.

Not possible, he surmised. *She's just a child. Maybe she kissed a boy, or she might even have a suitor she's waiting for.*

Malcolm had been that way with Jewel. He met her when he and Paw went to do some work at Mister Mason's farm. It was potato-picking time and Mister Mason needed extra hands to work. Jewel and her family were sharecroppers living on the Mason Farm. Jewel was older than Malcolm, with long legs, big breasts, and a big, round rear end. She always managed to brush against Malcolm while working in the field, pulling on potatoes. Her breasts would jiggle while she worked, revealing themselves through her sweaty blouse. This aroused Malcolm, along with the way that Jewel would hike her skirt up when she kneeled on the ground to work. Malcolm tried not to look, but his manhood took over. His Paw had warned him about the field hand girls. Paw didn't need any extra mouths to feed.

One day, while working on Mister Mason's farm, the rain suddenly came down hard, with screaming winds and thunder. Everyone working the fields scattered like scared mice. Out of nowhere, someone grabbed Malcolm's hand and commanded him to run fast. It was long-legged Jewel. With hair flying and breasts bouncing, Jewel moved quickly, with Malcolm in tow. Once inside an old, dilapidated barn, they ran and fell to ground.

Soaked from the hard rain, Malcolm saw Jewel disrobe from her wet clothes. She instructed him to do the same before he caught his death from a cold. Malcolm removed his garments with lightning speed. He had once caught a quick glimpse of his Mama naked, but it was nothing like watching Jewel, with her nice, full breasts and hard, black nipples at full attention. There was so much darkness below her waist that it looked like a full head of hair.

Jewel walked toward her and looked at his manhood. "Nice," she said. "Wasn't expecting such a large thing from a little boy."

"I ain't no boy," Malcolm confidently announced.

"Well, do you know how to use that thing since you ain't no boy?"

Malcolm choked on his words, his confidence waning. "Yeah, I have used it plenty of times," he said, his voice wavering.

"Well," Jewel seductively whispered in his ear, "my man, I guess you get to use it one more time."

Malcolm had never been with a naked woman before. He had

dry-f—ked plenty of times, but this was so much better—different, but better. He figured it had to be the same process. Jewel positioned herself on the ground with her thick, smooth brown legs wide open, and her bush fully exposed.

As soon as Malcolm mounted her, Jewel wrapped her long legs around him, rolled him over, and straddled him, taking control. This was Malcolm's first sexual experience.

Tulip turned to Malcolm with a questioning glance. "Why you smiling? Why you keep looking at me? I see you peeking at me, and I don't like it," she said.

"I don't mean nothing by it, Tulip. I guess I just like looking at you," Malcolm added.

Tulip was puzzled. She didn't understand. *But why?* Tulip questioned herself. *Do I look funny? Is something wrong with me? I know I am not clean as I should be, and my hair is a mess. I know I probably smell, but so does he. In fact, I'm cleaner than him.*

"What do you mean, you like looking at me?" she demanded, "Is there something wrong with me?" Tulip became agitated.

"I don't know," Malcolm said, surprised by her defensiveness. "I'll stop looking at you, alright?

"Let's start looking for a place to settle down. It'll be dark soon, and looks like the weather may turn. My leg's starting to bother me, too," said Malcolm, finding excuses to change the subject.

Tulip still wanted to know why Malcolm liked looking at her. *He thinks I'm a play toy,* she thought. *No, that's not it,* she decided.

It wasn't a bad look, like Papa Betts's evil gaze. In fact, it was rather pleasant. Tulip smiled to herself at the thought, before stealing a quick look at Malcolm. He was a rather handsome boy—maybe even a man, not that she had anyone to compare him to. She had met a few of the field hands' sons when their Papas stopped by to do some chores for Mama. But they were mean boys. Tulip remembered when one of the field hands stopped by with his two boys to patch their roof. Mama would trade some of her garden vegetables for work around the house that neither she nor Tulip could do. It was a necessary and fair trade.

Most of the men that stopped by inquired about Papa. Mama, being a woman of good sense, would never let on that he had gone home to heaven, but instead said he was away in town on business. She would notice that some of the men would give her a long look because she was a fair-complexioned woman, with long, black hair, deep-set black eyes, full lips, a narrow nose, and a nicely shaped body. As a young girl, Mama had been fondled, touched, and forced to perform sex acts. It seemed that, as a Negro girl, if you looked halfway decent, you would be abused, even by men in your own family. *Mama said that I would look like her one day, so I had to be careful around menfolk, but I really didn't understand why, until Mister Betts's farm.*

Tulip recalled an incident. She had been down by the river washing clothes, and noticed two boys watching her. One was around her age, maybe nine or ten. The other was a few years older. Mama and the field hand were talking near the barn. Tulip was walking back from the river with the clean wash. Her next chore was to drape the linens over the old twine line to dry. Before she knew it, the older boy had covered her mouth with one of his dirty hands and was using his other hand to fondle her Secret. He smelled of dog shit, and his breath was foul. He grabbed her hard and rough. Tulip tried to resist, but he was so much stronger. The younger boy just looked on with his mouth wide-open. Tulip kicked, twisted and struggled until the boy released her. She screamed as loud as she could. Mama and the field hand came running together.

"What is it, child?" Mama had asked. Tulip could only stare at the older boy with tears streaming down her face.

He answered for her. "We heard her scream and came running. We don't know what was wrong with her. Ain't that right, Sam?" he asked his little brother.

"Yea, that's right," the younger boy said, with his head hanging down.

Tulip looked at them both and ran to her house. She was embarrassed and confused by what had happened.

That was her first introduction to boys. She never told Mama. The next man to touch her would be Papa Betts and his friends. She had heard the expression, "Three times and you're out." Would her third encounter with a boy be just as cruel? Tulip decided that she didn't care much for boys or men. They were always hurting her.

But that wasn't really true. Within a short span of time, she had met a man and a boy who didn't want to hurt her. They only wanted to help her and keep her safe.

Her head began to hurt. It was all very confusing. Why do some men and boys hurt you, while some are kind to you? *I wish Mama was here to help me understand.* How could she trust this boy, Malcolm? In the beginning, he had not been very nice to her, but she knew that was because he had lost his Paw and was hurt and sad. But, since they had been traveling on the road, Malcolm had been nice to her and very protective—and sweet Jesus, this boy made her stomach feel funny when he touched her. Tulip didn't understand, but he felt like family. Malcolm had become her protector, and for that, she was thankful.

Tulip looked at Malcolm's muscular shoulders and strong arms. His skin was black as night. His lips were full, and his eyes were kind. Tulip liked looking at Malcolm. Was it possible he was sweet on her?

Mama, help me understand what's happening here. Could this be love?
Tulip waited.

> *My, the web we weave.*
> *Like raindrops from the heaven,*
> *feelings will multiply and spread.*
> *Like flowers that bloom, so will we.*
> *Like birds that sing, our love will be a fine melody.*
> *Like fish that swim, we move in spirit as one.*
> *Like sunrises and the moon that sets,*
> *up and down or even round and round the feeling will flow,*
> *but for sure no one but us knows that our love is like,*
> *a birth becomes brand new, welcoming,*
> *wanting, experiencing, exploring, needing,*
> *and praying that, like a life that's given,*
> *it should not be taken.*
> *So love, love, and be not deceived.*

chapter seventeen

First Time

"Malcolm!" called Tulip.

"Yeah, Tulip, what is it?" Malcolm was getting weary. They had been on the road now for weeks, maybe close to a month without a horse since Maggie had succumbed to illness roughly two weeks into their journey. They had received some food and water from the some of the farmhouses along the way, but many were filled with poor people without much to offer. Regardless, Tulip and Malcolm were grateful for any handouts they received.

Some kind folks, both colored and white, would give them a lift for a few miles and point them in the direction of the big city, New York. While walking along, Tulip and Malcolm encountered the strong smell of smoke. The odor engulfed the air and gave off a stench. As they walked along, they saw a small sign that read, "Mining Town, Elmira, New York, Pop. 1500."

"Finally, a town," Malcolm said out loud. "Maybe we can find some work so we can earn some money for food and shelter." They picked up speed on their way to the town, excited at the prospect of what they might find.

Elmira, New York was an upcoming coal mining town. It had dirt roads with makeshift rows of houses built close together with wood plank porches. A cloud of smoke hung over the town, giving it a dark, hazy look, and a unique odor. Most of the men and young boys in the town worked in the mines retrieving coal, which was sold to businesses and houses for heat and cooking. Working in the coal mine was hard, long and dangerous, but it provided money for food and housing. White men and a few colored men worked in the coal mines, though not many colored folk lived in the town.

As they entered the town, Tulip and Malcolm looked at each other and held their noses from the awful smell. They coughed as thick smoke entered their lungs. Malcolm could see people moving about, and was eager to ask for work.

Tulip noticed the white men looking at her. For some reason, their stares made her shake in fear. Tulip tugged at Malcolm's shirt.

"What is it, Tulip?" Malcolm asked with irritation.

"I can't breathe. I don't like it here. Let's go back to the road," murmured Tulip.

"But we need to find work to earn money for our travels to New York City," said Malcolm, frustrated with Tulip's childish behavior. They needed money, but more importantly, Malcolm's leg needed tending. He was weak and his leg had become discolored and swollen. The pain was tolerable, but his leg needed looking after. Tulip had done her best to treat him, but she was not a doctor. Malcolm knew that he needed help sooner than later.

He also knew that the seasons were changing. The weather was getting cooler, which meant that winter was coming. Even though winters in the South were not bitterly cold, they could be unpredictable. Neither he nor Tulip had proper clothing or rations for a sudden change in the weather. Malcolm recalled that, as a youth, he had experienced several harsh snow storms. He needed to get Tulip settled somewhere so that he could move on, and maybe Elmira was the place.

Deep in thought, Malcolm did not realize that Tulip was no longer walking behind him. She had stopped walking toward the town and had turned back to the road. Throwing his hands up in frustration, Malcolm turned and joined her.

Tulip and Malcolm had been on the road for weeks. They were able to get some rations from several farms, and even found fruit trees and wild berries. Malcolm said that he had seen a sign that said that Albany, New York was about 200 miles ahead.

"I'm tired and cold," Tulip complained. "Let's go into the forest and make camp for the night." Malcolm agreed.

Together, Tulip and Malcolm worked to prepare a camp. There was a gentle breeze in the air, and the leaves were falling quietly to the ground, letting them know that a change was coming. The forest was quiet and still, except for the gentle swaying of the trees, as if they were dancing to music. Malcolm gathered tree limbs to make a fire, while Tulip prepared some wild greens for their supper.

Tulip had caught a chill, and there was not enough clothing or bedding to keep them both warm. The fire would help, but Tulip was concerned.

Malcolm put a pot with water on the fire for Tulip to cook the wild greens. The cured meat was long gone, but there was still a little salt left. They had to make do. They ate the greens and sat huddled together, close to the fire to keep warm.

The nightfall brought with it a sudden drop in temperature, which went from cool to cold quickly. Malcolm saw that Tulip was shivering. "Come closer," he nudged.

Tulip hesitated. She was not comfortable being so close to Malcolm. She trusted him and knew that he wouldn't harm her, but she still felt uneasy.

"Tulip," Malcolm insisted, "We need to be close to keep warm.

Come." He was firm, but gentle.

Tulip sheepishly moved closer.

Malcolm saw the uncertainty and mistrust in her eyes. It made him wonder what had happened to cause her to be so fearful. Hoping not to frighten her any further, Malcolm slowly put his arms around Tulip and moved her closer to him. Together, they sat close to the fire without saying a word or making any eye contact, listening to the sounds of night.

Sometime in the middle of the night, Malcolm woke to find Tulip nestled under him. He looked at her and gently stoked her face. *She is really pretty*, Malcolm thought. He felt his manhood stir. *Hey—none of that, she's just a child*, Malcolm thought to himself. Still, he moved in closer and continued stroking Tulip's face. Just touching her made Malcolm heat up, both inside and out. He no longer felt the cold of the night, only the heat of passion.

Tulip felt the nearness of Malcolm: it felt warm and peaceful. It made her think of home and happier times before she was on her own. *Mama, Mama, I feel so nice and warm.* Tulip turned to face Malcolm, and it was as if he was staring directly into her soul. She felt the depths of him, if that was even possible. No words were spoken between them. Tulip didn't know what to expect, but this was different from Papa Betts.

Malcolm kissed her lips so gently that it brought tears to Tulip's eyes. She shivered.

Malcolm whispered softly, "I won't hurt you and I'll stop if you want me to."

Tulip didn't want him to stop. Malcolm kissed her nose, her forehead, her eyes, and her cheeks.

He nibbled her ears, which made her shiver, but not from the cold. This was an unfamiliar feeling. Malcolm slowly made his way through Tulip's layers of clothing. Her legs were long, soft and strong. Malcolm rubbed them slowly.

Tulip wanted more, and she made a soft cry of pleasure. She held on tightly to Malcolm, a little timid. This felt right and good. She felt a wetness in her Secret unlike any other she remembered. Her body responded in ways it never had. Was it possible that Malcolm loved her and she loved him? Could this be true love—the love that Mama said that she would have one day? Tulip looked up to the sky and smiled.

Malcolm entered Tulip with his manhood slowly and gently. He wanted to push harder, but he didn't want to hurt her. Most of all, he didn't want to rush it.

As he entered the tight, warm, wet haven between her legs, he knew there was no turning back. Tulip accepted him as if it was the most natural thing. At first, there was some pain, but as she relaxed, her Secret became engulfed in pleasure. *My God*, she wanted to yell. *Yes! Yes!* Tulip moaned, wrapping her legs around his lower body, moving with him in motion. It was pure, and it was beautiful.

Malcolm could no longer refrain, and exploded in sheer pleasure. His rhythm slowed, and his motion stopped. He was still.

More, more. Tulip wanted to yell to Malcolm, "Please don't stop!" She felt out of control. Papa Betts and his friends had hurt her, but Malcolm felt good. She was on the edge of something more powerful, but Malcolm stopped.

If a song could be written about Tulip and Malcolm's first night together, it would be one of shooting stars and rain showers. How fragile they were! The feeling that they encountered was the pure nature of two souls drawn together. They no longer felt cold as they slept together. There was no denying that this was love. Under that light of night and God's promise, Tulip and Malcolm were wrapped together, be it right or wrong.

They slept until they felt gentle snowflakes on their faces. Tulip suddenly sat up and thought, *What's happening?* She looked around through foggy eyes and found that the forest was white and beautiful. *Am I in heaven?* Tulip wondered. *Did our loving bring this on?* It was peaceful and still.

"Malcolm, Malcolm," Tulip called as she shook him. "Wake up, you got to see!" she exclaimed.

Malcolm rubbed his eyes and leaned back on his elbows. "Wow! It's snowing," Malcolm said. "It's snowing," Malcolm repeated, as if he found it hard to comprehend.

Tulip and Malcolm rose to their feet together. She felt a sudden rush and a little soreness between her legs. It was a sudden reminder of their night together.

"Malcolm, this is so beautiful," Tulip said. "I really love the snow. This must be a gift from Mama for me to remember home." Tulip smiled to herself. It reminded her of growing up in the snowy, cold winters of Connecticut. Tulip twirled around, scooped up a handful snow and ate a big patch.

"Hey," Malcolm said, "You not supposed to eat the first snow."

"What? "Why?" Tulip was puzzled.

Malcolm explained that his Granny had always said that the first snow was dirty and should not be eaten. Tulip laughed, threw a handful of snow at Malcolm, and ran off in delight.

My, My, love is such a beautiful thing.
So free, so easy, no regrets.
How we welcome with our hearts our feeling
and need for another person to share with us the pleasures of life.
So here we are, two people, now trying to become one and not

fearing that we will not be able live without the other, no frets.

My, My, love is such a wonderful gift.
It comes ready and willing.
Not a thought is given to why this is happening with this person.
The here and now is what is most important.
His smile, her laugh, his eyes, her mouth, his touch, her readiness.
No denying or refusal, just pure giving.

My, My, love is such a state of being.
No one knows when it will start or how or if will end.
Because there is no set time period on this ride of emotion or need.
It may come in waves or leave with the storm.
But, the in between is the strongest.

chapter eighteen

Bridge Over Troubled Waters

"$\mathscr{I}$t looks like there's a house across the river," Tulip said, as she turned to look in Malcolm's direction a few days later.

Tulip used her hand to shade her eyes for a better look. Malcolm was lazily relaxing by the riverbank. Between walking on a bad leg and loving Tulip at night, his energy needed to be recharged. Malcolm rose up on his elbows to look in the direction that Tulip was pointing. Sure enough, through the dense forest, the leaves had fallen from the trees, providing a view of what lay beyond.

"Yes," Malcolm said, "I see the house. But we can't go through the water and get wet. We would freeze. Maybe if we follow the river down farther we'll find a path to the other side."

"Malcolm, I'm so hungry. Please, we must try," Tulip pleaded.

"You're always hungry." teased Malcolm. "Hungry and Sleepy are your new names," he laughed.

Tulip playfully hit Malcolm has he ran about.

"Okay, enough playing," said Malcolm. The food was gone, and they had taken to foraging what they could from the forest.

"Okay, let's pack up everything," Malcolm announced. "It might be a long walk, and we don't want to have to double back if it's dark."

Tulip hurriedly packed their few belongings. Malcolm helped to stomp out the fire and they proceeded to walk along the riverside. Through the trees, they could see a few horses, some pigs, and a cow. There was smoke coming from the house chimney. They even thought that they heard the laughter of children. Tulip and Malcolm looked at each other and smiled. They began to walk faster, almost running. It felt like it had been weeks since they had seen another person.

The river appeared to be going on forever, and the house and farm were getting farther and farther away. Malcolm thought they needed to make a raft to get to the other side, but he would need rope and a saw to cut the wood.

Tulip spotted it first. Malcolm looked up ahead and saw that there was a rope bridge to get to the other side. Tulip and Malcolm ran as fast as they could with their bundles. The bridge was made with thick rope and rotting boards. It appeared to be very stable, but Malcolm was not certain. What if the rope snapped from their weight? Or what if one of the boards gave way? They would land in the cold river and be swept away. He didn't know if Tulip could swim.

Malcolm turned to Tulip. "Give me your bundles and let me cross first. If it can hold my weight and the bundles, then you'll be safe to cross. Can you swim?"

"I don't know," Tulip replied with a puzzled look.

Malcolm took that as a "no."

"Why can't we go together?" Tulip asked desperately. "I don't want to be left alone."

"I am not leaving you alone," Malcolm reasoned. "I just want to make sure the bridge is strong enough for us both to cross. If it breaks, I can swim back to you," Malcolm said, as calmly as he could.

Tulip wasn't sure, but she had to trust Malcolm's decision. She was scared to be without him. What if the bridge broke and he drowned? What would she do without him? She didn't want to lose him.

Seeing that Tulip was hesitant, Malcolm gently tilted her head and softly kissed her lips. With that, he lifted the bundles to his back and started a slow walk across the bridge.

The bridge was old and made of rope and planks of wood. There were gaps at least six inches wide between each plank, with wider gaps in some places, so that you would have to be careful of your steps. The sides consisted of long, fraying ropes that swung loosely. The crudely-made bridge stretched from one side of the river to the other, high above the water. Malcolm moved deliberately across the bridge, careful of his footing. The bridged swayed with his weight. Malcolm didn't want to chance looking back at Tulip for fear that he might miss his footing and fall between the decaying wood floor planks. The river below the bridge was moving swiftly and made a loud sound. The wind was picking up with a cold breeze.

Malcolm continued forward. He estimated that the bridge was just short of six hundred feet from one side to the other. Once he reached the other side, he would call for Tulip to cross the bridge. He was fearful for her, but it was a chance that they had to take.

Malcolm gripped the ropes on either side of the bridge, calculating each step. Water from the river splashed his face, giving him a chill, but he moved on. A few times, he missed his footing and some of the wood planks chipped away, but he kept moving. Finally, Malcolm stepped off the bridge onto dry land on the other side.

Malcolm could barely see Tulip, but she was waving and yelling at him. He just sat there for a few minutes. A mixture of thoughts ran through his head. He could cut the bridge and be free of her, or simply run off. He was frozen in his negative thoughts.

"Malcolm! Malcolm!" Tulip yelled. What was he doing? Why hadn't he signaled for her to cross? Maybe it wasn't safe. What would happen to her if Malcolm didn't wait for her to cross? "*Malcolm! Malcolm!*" Tulip yelled, close to hysterics.

Someone was calling him. Malcolm shook his head. What was he thinking? *Tulip!* Malcolm jumped to his feet and dropped the bundles on his back. He yelled and waved at Tulip.

"The bridge is safe, come on across! Hold on tight to each side and please watch your step! Tulip, move very slowly!'

Tulip heard Malcolm and wiped her tear-stained face. *I knew he wouldn't leave me. He loves me.*

Tulip slowly stepped onto the bridge. She looked down at the rushing water below her feet and felt lightheaded. It felt as though she was moving with the river. The water splashing on her caused her to shiver. She moved slowly.

Malcolm yelled, "Tulip, don't look down and move very slowly! I am waiting for you! Come on, you can do this!"

Tulip couldn't answer Malcolm. The bridge was swaying with the wind. Tulip stopped moving. Frozen in fear, she couldn't take another step. "Mama! Mama! Help me," prayed Tulip.

Tulip, Tulip, look at the flowers waiting for you on the other side. Smell the perfume from their scent. Come, my precious child, and join me with the flowers.

Tulip opened her eyes. Just ahead, she could see different hues of flowers. She smelled the sweet fragrance and slowly began to move.

Malcolm was tempted to run onto the bridge and pull Tulip across. He saw her frozen in fear, but then, slowly, she began to move.

"Tulip," Malcolm called out patiently. His heart was beating through his chest. "Come to me, you can do it. You're almost here.

Come on girly."

Malcolm called to Tulip with his arms stretched out toward her. *Come to me, my love.* He not want to think of what would happen if Tulip lost her grip and fell into the rushing water below. He could not lose her. She was now his family.

Hearing the love in Malcolm's voice, Tulip regained her composure and slowly began to proceed down the bridge to her love. Tulip's eyes filled with tears because she knew that she felt love, and it was giving her the courage and strength she needed. As Tulip finally approached, he could not restrain himself any longer. He reached out and grabbed Tulip, pulling her the remaining distance across the bridge. They fell into each other's embrace. Malcolm held her tightly. No words were needed.

So they say ain't no mountain high enough
or river wide enough to keep me from my love.
What is a bridge that must be crossed to reach the path one must
take to find its true heart?
Can a bridge be too high or too wide to get two hearts from
becoming one…?

A bridge can only be in time or just a figment of our mind,
But, for our love to come together, it must grow.
The longer it takes to cross,
the farther away the love will go…

Therefore, I say to you my love,
this bridge will not stop me from giving you my trust,
from giving you my heart, and maybe one day, together,
we will cross this bridge as one.

chapter nineteen

Helping Hands

"Come, Tulip, we need to move down the river before night falls. The house we saw should be no more than a mile or so away."

Looking back at the bridge, Tulip couldn't believe that she had crossed it. "Thank you, Mama," she said to herself.

Quickly, Tulip and Malcolm gathered their bundles. They began to walk through the thick forest littered with hanging tree limbs and overgrown shrubs. Walking carefully, Malcolm called out to Tulip, who was following closely behind. He turned around to see if Tulip was keeping up.

"Look down as you walk because there may be snakes or traps," Malcolm said calmly.

Tulip's eyes opened wide with fear.

"No need to be afraid, just be careful." Malcolm didn't want to scare her, but he sensed that this side of the river was a little different from the other side.

Together, Tulip and Malcolm moved through the dense forest. Night was quickly approaching.

"How much farther, Malcolm?" Tulip asked.

"I am not sure, but it shouldn't be too much farther. Let's just move a little faster. We need to find the house before nightfall."

As soon as Malcolm spoke, they heard a deep voice loudly commanding them not to take another step.

Tulip and Malcolm stopped dead in their tracks. They didn't know whether or not to put their hands up, and they didn't dare turn around. Malcolm began to speak.

"We are just looking for a little food and place to rest for the night. We mean no harm or disrespect. We've been travelling the roads for weeks and lost our sense of time. We don't have any weapons. We're just hungry and tired."

Tulip didn't say a word. She was frozen with fear and flashes of what had happened at the Betts Farm. She would rather die than go through that again.

There was no movement and no noise. There was just silence for what seemed like a lifetime. Would they be killed right then and there? They both stood still, waiting for a response.

Finally, the voice said, "Turn around and follow me, and nothing funny. If so, I will shoot the both of you like I'm hunting rabbits."

With bowed heads, both Tulip and Malcolm turned around. *What a sight they were*, the man thought. Dirty, ragged, nappy-headed, and stinky. Both were young, or at least the girl was. The man wasn't sure about this tall, lanky boy.

Tulip and Malcolm turned around to see a giant of a man. He was a tall, black man with a head full of thick, brown hair. He had very dark eyes and a wide smile. He motioned to Tulip and Malcolm to follow him. Malcolm looked at Tulip and saw her hesitation, but they had no choice. They had to trust this man. If not, they would starve in these woods.

Malcolm began to follow the man, who was moving quickly through the forest. His long legs covered a lot of ground quickly.

"Come on in here and shut the door. Y'all gone let critters in."

They entered the house with Tulip gripping Malcolm's arm tightly. The door closed behind them with a loud bang. Tulip jumped and beads of sweat appeared on her forehead. Tulip recalled the horrors of the last house she was invited into.

Tulip and Malcolm saw a petite white woman with long, yellow hair and blue eyes. Her hair hung in soft, loose curls. Her skin, although white, had a look as though the sun had kissed it, maybe from the years of harvesting her crops.

But didn't the colored man call her his love? Malcolm thought to himself. Malcolm looked further into the house and saw three children quietly sitting at a long wooden table, looking at him and Tulip. There were three pretty little girls, looking like a smaller version of their mother, with the same yellow hair, blue eyes, and tanned skin.

"Papa, who are they?" one of the girls asked, with all the curiosity of a seven-year-old child. Tulip and Malcolm looked at the children and then their mother. It was confusing. *How could a black man be the Pa of these mulatto children?* Of course, they had seen mulattos before, but it was always the Papa who was white.

Sensing their reservation, the pretty lady motioned for Tulip and Malcolm to sit at the table with the girls. The three girls followed Tulip and Malcolm with their eyes.

"Let me get you two some of this nice, hot squirrel stew to warm your insides", the lady said. The lady motioned toward two open spots on the bench.

"Here," she motioned. "Sit while I get you two something to eat. My, my, look at you two!

"Oh, where are my manners? I'm May, May Chiles. That handsome man, you just met is my husband, Mister Noel Chiles," she chuckled, "and these three are our daughters: Faith, who's the oldest at nine, Hope, seven, and baby Charity, who is three.

"Faith, Hope and Charity," said the Chiles children in chorus.

"Girls, say hello to our guests."

The girls greeted the two, again in unison.

"Now, who do we have the pleasure of joining us?"

Malcolm stepped forward.

"My name is Malcolm Thornton and this here is Tulip."

"Well, nice to meet you, Malcolm and Tulip, and welcome to our home. We wash our hands and pray before supper, so I'll have my Faith show you where to wash up. Then we can pray and eat this meal that God has blessed us with."

Faith led Tulip and Malcolm to a bucket of water and handed them a piece of soap that smelled medicinal. Tulip's Mama used to make lye soap. She smiled as she washed her hands and thought of her.

Tulip and Malcolm watched the food as Faith helped Misses Chiles top plates with hot biscuits and gravy, meat, white potatoes, wild greens, brown beans, and fresh lemonade to wash it down. Malcolm looked and Tulip and smiled.

They both sat with their hands folded in their laps while two plates were placed in front of them. They looked around at the mixed family. Malcolm had heard about white and black people loving each other, but this his first time he had seen them actually married. *No time to be concerned about that,* Malcolm thought as he hungrily looked at that food before him.

The family joined hands, linking Tulip and Malcolm's, as well. Mister Chiles began, "Lord, our Father, we first give thanks for your blessings with the food before us. We are humble, and we are thankful. We also like to give thanks to you bringing two guests to our humble home. May they feel welcomed. With that, Lord, we thank you. Amen.

"Okay," Mister Chiles said. "My love, you have prepared a wonderful meal and we thank you."

"Thank you, but as always, Faith lent a helping hand," said Misses Chiles, smiling at her daughter.

"Well, my thanks to you, too, daughter," nodded Mister Chiles.

Faith blushed and Mister Chiles and Misses Chiles looked at each other and smiled. Tulip and Malcolm looked at them a bit confused, because they had never seen such a display of affection between a man and woman.

As the food was passed around the table, Tulip and Malcolm only put small amounts on their plates, so as not to appear greedy. But Misses Chiles added more to their plates at every opportunity, and smiled. Together, Tulip and Malcolm ate until their stomachs could hold no more.

After supper, Tulip helped Misses Chiles and her girls clear the table. Leftover scraps were placed outside for Max.

Mister Chiles carried Max's scraps out of the house to the wood-planked porch, beckoning Malcolm to follow him. He told Malcolm to have a seat in one of the two rocking chairs. Mister Chiles sat in the remaining chair. After Max finished his scraps, he laid down next to Mister Chiles and let out a satisfied sigh. Mister Chiles retrieved his pipe and tobacco from his front shirt pocket, filled the pipe with tobacco, and lit it up for a smoke.

"Malcolm, I don't know your story, son, but you been respectful. I know people and I know you won't bring no trouble around here. You and Tulip are welcome to stay here tonight. It's too dangerous to be in those woods at night."

"We do appreciate it," Malcolm said, "but we don't want to be any trouble. You and your wife have been more than kind."

Hearing Malcolm talk, Tulip turned and smiled in his direction.

Tulip thought about how nice this was, to have a home, a husband, and children. Maybe, one day, she and Malcolm would have a beautiful home and family. Tulip turned to look to see Misses Chiles smiling at her. *How pretty she is*, Tulip thought, *but she is a white woman with a black man.*

After finishing the dishes, Misses Chiles helped the girls prepare for bed. The girls came in their nighties to kiss their Papa goodnight. Mister Chiles excused himself from Tulip and Malcolm to join Misses Chiles in their nightly prayers with the girls.

Tulip sat close to Malcolm, by the fire. They just sat there, in their own thoughts, looking at the fire. Seeing their expressions, Mister and Misses Chiles hugged and watched Tulip and Malcolm. Sensing their presence, Malcolm jumped to his feet.

"Didn't mean to startle you" said Mister Chiles, "but, my love and I were thinking about how much you two remind us of us when we were your age."

Tulip and Malcolm both blushed. "Thank you," Malcolm said, "for the food, and opening your home to us."

"No need to thank us," Misses Chiles said lovingly. "Now, let's get you two settled for night."

Up in the barn loft, Tulip and Malcolm cuddled close together and felt thankful for a helping hand. Content, they drifted off into Dreamland.

Tulip woke up, rubbed her eyes and stretched out her arms wide. She had not slept that well, it seemed, in years. She turned to wake Malcolm, but he was not there. Tulip panicked.

"Malcolm!" she called. *He left me, he left me!* Tears streamed down her face, and then she heard voices. Tulip looked over the loft and could see Malcolm and Mister Chiles shaking hands. Tulip began to gather her bundle and blankets to give back to Misses Chiles.

"G'morning, Tulip!" Malcolm came up to the loft and grabbed Tulip excitedly. "Good News! Mister Chiles wants to hire me to help him with some work. We can stay here until we have enough money to move on."

Tulip stared at Malcolm.

Could it be that life has taken a different turn?
Could it be that now, we begin our time with each other?
Could it be by chance that we may be what dreams are all about?
Could it be that a door has closed and a new door has opened?
Could it be...

chapter twenty

Building Together

*M*alcolm and Tulip settled in at the Chiles Farm. They even got comfortable with seeing a Negro man with a white woman. The Chiles's children were home-schooled by Misses Chiles, so when Tulip finished helping Misses Chiles with washing, cooking, and picking crops, she would sit in on lessons about reading, numbers, and writing. Tulip was a very quick learner. She recognized a few words from her Bible teaching with Mama, but she enjoyed learning new words, and even learned how to write her name and count to one hundred. It made Tulip feel smart like Malcolm, who could already read and write.

Life on the Chiles's farm was easy. Months flew by quickly. Tulip missed Malcolm when he went away with Mister Chiles to find work. Sometimes, they would be gone for weeks. During those times, Tulip would play with the Chiles's children, especially Faith, whom she was quite fond of. Misses Chiles also helped make clothes for Tulip and Malcolm. Tulip had Misses Chiles purchase cloth with some of the money that Malcolm made. Tulip was proud of the dresses she made for herself and wanted to look nice for Malcolm.

Since arriving at the Chiles farm, Tulip's monthly bleeding had stopped. Mama had told her that it would come every thirty days, and it was God's way of making a woman different from a man.

Tulip knew that she was young, but she had become a woman by then, so maybe the bleeding stopped because God knew that, too. The bleeding had been uncomfortable, and her stomach hurt every time it came.

Tulip wanted to ask Misses Chiles about the bleeding, but was much too embarrassed to talk about such a private thing. Malcolm poked Tulip's stomach and told her that the good food was getting her fat in the middle. Tulip had to admit that she was hungry most of time, but she believed that this was because she had been starving since Mama died. Now, being able to have plenty of food, she just wanted to eat.

Tulip smiled to herself when she thought of the biscuits and bacon that Misses Chiles would cook. Her mouth watered, and she yearned for a nice hot biscuit with plenty of butter and crispy bacon. If Malcolm knew her thoughts, he would tease her for being so greedy and always thinking about food. The thought of food also made Tulip sleepy—that's another thing: she was always sleepy. Sometimes, while out in the fields digging in the dirt for potatoes, Tulip would lie down for a quick nap. Tulip could not get enough sleep. Eat and sleep were small pleasures, but having Malcolm love her, touch her Secret, and kiss her breasts was better than sleep and food on any day.

Tulip realized that even her dreams of Mama were less frequent. It was not that she didn't love Mama anymore, but she didn't feel alone now that she had Malcolm. She still missed Mama, but Malcolm was now her family. *Mama would have liked Malcolm*, thought Tulip. He had good manners, was kind, and he loved Jesus. She wished that Mama was alive to meet Malcolm. Tulip closed her eyes and could see the field of flowers—so sweet, so beautiful. In the distance, she heard her name being called.

Malcolm didn't want to lose the man, so he turned quickly and grabbed Tulip's hand so that they could move together. Night had fallen, but the man continued to move toward the lights of a house that was not far in the distance. Keeping up with the man proved to very challenging for both Tulip and Malcolm, but they had no other choice.

The man began to slow down as he reached a barbed wire fence. He kept walking down a long dirt path. Tulip and Malcolm noticed a large barn. Dogs were barking loudly.

"Come here, boy." The man summoned one of the animals.

A big, brown, tail-wagging dog ran up and immediately jumped on the man. Tulip eased behind Malcolm. The big brown dog jumped on Malcolm.

"Don't worry," the man said, "Max won't eat you unless I tell him to." With that, the man let out a loud laugh. Tulip and Malcolm did not see the humor. They held onto each other even more tightly.

With Max by his side, the man continued to walk up the dirt path toward the light coming from the house. Suddenly, the door opened, and a sweet voice called out, "Noel, is that you? Who is that with you?"

"Yes, it's me, my love, and I found two youngins over yonder in the woods. Brought them home for a meal and much-needed baths," The man announced.

"Well, hurry up, supper is getting cold."

The man reached the house and walked through the open door. Max ran off around the back of the house. Tulip and Malcolm stood still at the front door, leaving it slightly ajar. Their stomachs growled from the smell of good food. They could feel the warmth coming from inside of the house, but they dared not enter until properly invited.

"Come on in here and shut the door. Y'all gone let critters in."

They entered the house with Tulip gripping Malcolm's arm tightly. The door closed behind them with a loud bang. Tulip jumped and beads of sweat appeared on her forehead. Tulip recalled the horrors of the last house she was invited into.

Tulip and Malcolm saw a petite white woman with long, yellow hair and blue eyes. Her hair hung in soft, loose curls. Her skin, although white, had a look as though the sun had kissed it, maybe from the years of harvesting her crops.

But didn't the colored man call her his love? Malcolm thought to himself. Malcolm looked further into the house and saw three children quietly sitting at a long wooden table, looking at him and Tulip. There were three pretty little girls, looking like a smaller version of their mother, with the same yellow hair, blue eyes, and tanned skin.

"Papa, who are they?" one of the girls asked, with all the curiosity of a seven-year-old child. Tulip and Malcolm looked at the children and then their mother. It was confusing. *How could a black man be the Pa of these mulatto children?* Of course, they had seen mulattos before, but it was always the Papa who was white.

Sensing their reservation, the pretty lady motioned for Tulip and Malcolm to sit at the table with the girls. The three girls followed Tulip and Malcolm with their eyes.

"Let me get you two some of this nice, hot squirrel stew to warm your insides", the lady said. The lady motioned toward two open spots on the bench.

"Here," she motioned. "Sit while I get you two something to eat. My, my, look at you two!

"Oh, where are my manners? I'm May, May Chiles. That handsome man, you just met is my husband, Mister Noel Chiles,"

"Tulip!"

She jumped at the sound of her name. "Am I dreaming?" Tulip said aloud. "Did someone call my name?"

"Tulip! Tulip!" Malcolm called out.

Tulip was laying in the barn loft where she and Malcolm had made their home. She jumped up.

"Yes, Malcolm. I'm coming." Tulip stuck her head out of the loft's window and allowed the ends of her lips to curl, resulting in a flirtatious smile. "Why you yelling my name like a crazy man?"

"There you are, girl. How would you like to kick up your heels and go dancing with your man?" Malcolm asked, grinning in her direction and looking as handsome as ever. Working with Mister Chiles and having good food had caused Malcolm to add weight to his tall frame. His muscles were noticeable under his shirt. His skin was like nice, smooth chocolate. His body was hard and lean.

"What do mean, kick up my heels? You been drinking again?" Tulip asked sternly. "Or, have you lost your marbles?"

"Dance, girl! Haven't you ever been dancing?" Malcolm asked, smiling. "Some fellas told be about a dance tonight, not too far from here. I asked Mister Chiles if I could use the buggy to take you dancing. He thought it was a damn good idea. He said we're young and should get out and have fun," he added with pride. Malcolm showed off his dance moves.

Tulip couldn't believe her eyes. *Dancing?* she said to herself. *I've never danced with anyone.* She and Mama used to run around the house and pretend to dance. But Tulip was nervous at the thought of dancing in public.

"I don't know."

"Tulip! What you say? Do I have a date? Would you do me the honor, my pretty lady?" Malcolm asked, bowing.

Tulip felt her skin getting hot. *Malcolm has gone mad*, she thought. *A date? "Pretty lady?" What in the world?* She was exhausted. Flattered, but exhausted.

"Stop yelling, Malcolm," said Tulip. "You gonna scare everybody." *A date,* she thought. *I don't have nothing to wear on a date or to a dance.* Tulip turned her back to the window.

"Wait right there!" said Malcolm.

Now what? thought Tulip.

Malcolm came running through the barn door, causing the chickens to flap their wings as he rushed by them. Malcolm climbed the loft ladder two steps at a time. Tulip was standing there when he reached the top. Malcolm brought a sack from behind his back.

"Here. This is for you. A gift," Malcolm said shyly.

"A gift for me!" said Tulip. "I never had anyone give me a gift before." Her eyes glistened with tears, not reaching for the sack. "It's not my birthday, Malcolm."

"I know, but when I saw this, I thought of you," he said lovingly. "Here," he added, extending the sack to her.

Tulip looked at Malcolm. She felt such love for him. She looked at the sack, looked at Malcolm, and held out her hand to receive his gift. Slowly, she opened the sack and peeped inside, like she was afraid that something would reach out and bite her. What could this gift possibly be? As Tulip reached in the sack, she pulled out a pretty white dress with a blue ribbon and bows. It was the prettiest dress Tulip had ever seen. Tears rolled down her face.

"Misses Chiles helped me pick it out from the Sears, Roebuck Catalog where you can order stuff. I was saving it for a special occasion," Malcolm said, while lowering his head. "But, seeing that this would be our first date, this is good a time as any. Plus, you'll be the prettiest girl at the dance."

Tulip hugged Malcolm with all her might. "Thank You!"

In life, some things will be expected,
and others will come without any expectation;
Take care that it doesn't pass without seeing the natural beauty in
what was given instead of expecting;
Breath above water is expected, but not a given;
So, when it comes, treasure it, be thankful;
because it may be your last.

chapter twenty-one

Courting

*M*alcolm and Tulip rode along the tree-lined path, hardly saying a word to each other. The evening was calm, with a mystical feel, and the air was warm, with a slight crispness. No wildlife stirred, but the sounds of nature could be heard. Tulip felt beautiful, but her stomach was doing flip-flops. She was excited and nervous all in one. A dance, date, flowers, Malcolm, a beautiful dress, hair fixed with bows…what more could she want on this perfect evening? Malcolm even held her hand and helped her into the buggy, like a perfect gentleman. *He's so handsome*, thought Tulip, sneaking little peeks at him. *He's so pretty all cleaned-up.* Tulip giggled to herself.

"What are you laughing about?" said Malcolm, who was deep in thought about Tulip's transformation. *She's becoming quite a woman, and will be a good wife for some man. I have too much living to do to think about a wife. Too young to be a husband.*

Hopefully, he could save enough money to help Tulip get settled somewhere. That was his goal. He wanted to get her settled and be on his way. They both had a lot of living left to do. *We are still very young, and even though we have been intimate, I am not ready to be a husband*, pondered Malcolm. *Why am I thinking about such things right now? Tonight is a fun time, and we're young. We deserve it.*

Malcolm laughed aloud.

"Now what are *you* laughing about?" inquired Tulip.

"Oh, just enjoying the evening with my pretty girl," said Malcolm.

"How much farther do we have to go?" asked Tulip.

Malcolm responded, "This fella, his name is Jessie. We met when I went to town with Mister Chiles. He told me every third Saturday, after sundown, there's a dance for us colored folks in an old abandoned grain farm and all are welcomed. Jessie gave me the directions, so I figure we should be there soon. Jessie said we'll see folks on the road making their way to the dance."

Just as Malcolm finished speaking, a buggy with about six people—colored boys and girls—approached them at a fast pace. The buggy slowed down, and the driver came up to Malcolm's side.

"Hey, Malcolm! Is that you, boy? Look at you, Negro, all dapper down!" said Jessie, rather roughly and with a big grin. Jessie was a big boy, and tall for his age of nineteen. He had very dark skin, with full features and white teeth. He had very large hands and big, long feet. He wasn't a bad-looking boy.

Malcolm grinned. "Jessie, man, is that you with your Sunday best?"

"Yep," Jessie said as he slicked back his hair with his hand. The three girls in the buggy were looking Malcolm up and down and smiling. They had seen Malcolm around town and thought him to be a handsome and good man. The girls knew that he had a girl, so they also took a quick look at Tulip, whom they viewed as competition.

Tulip felt hot under the girls' gazes as they whispered to each other.

"Malcolm, who is that pretty little thing you got there?" asked

Jessie, smiling and eyeing Tulip up and down.

"This here is my girl, Tulip" replied Malcolm. "Tulip, this is Jessie."

"Pleased to meet you, sir," said Tulip.

With that, loud laughter came from Jessie's buggy. "*Pleased to meet you, sir,*" the girls said mockingly. Tulip turned red.

"Hey, Malcolm, we're almost there! Take a swig of this and follow me," Jessie said. He tossed a mason jar filled with brown liquor to Malcolm.

Malcolm had to quickly stand in the buggy, hold the horses' reins with one hand, and catch the container with the other hand, almost losing control of the buggy.

Tulip grabbed the reins so they wouldn't flip over. While Tulip held the reins, Malcolm raised the mason jar to his lips. "Ooh wee!" yelled Malcolm. "This some good s—t here."

Tulip looked up at Malcolm, surprised by his foul language. He looked at Tulip and offered her the jar. She shook her head.

"Oh, well. More for us, Jessie." Both Jessie and Malcolm laughed. The boys and girls in Jessie's wagon laughed, too. Tulip didn't see what was so funny.

Malcolm followed Jessie's buggy into a big field. There were a lot of wagons, other buggies and horses, even some automobiles. A lot of folks were moving about, laughing and talking. Tulip had never seen so many folks in one place before. Malcolm tied up the horses and helped Tulip to the ground. They walked toward the big barn, which was aglow with lights. The girls from Jessie's buggy ran in the same direction. Tulip wanted to run, as well, but she didn't want to leave Malcolm.

Malcolm, Jessie and the other boys were passing around the jar of moonshine. Tulip waited, tapping her foot to the music, as

Malcolm drank with them. She was annoyed and anxious to get to the dance.

As they got closer to the barn, they could hear music and singing. Folks were dancing both outside and inside. Tulip was so excited, she thought that she would burst.

Malcolm grabbed Tulip and turned her around so fast, she thought that she would faint from being dizzy, but she only laughed. The music reached Tulip's soul and her body responded. Mama had told Tulip she was a good dancer, but that was a child just jumping around. This music felt good and made Tulip want to *really* dance.

Before she knew it, she and Malcolm were in the middle of the floor and people were shouting "Go, baby, go!" That just made Tulip move faster.

Malcolm was amazed at how Tulip could dance. He had never seen her dance before. He had never before seen her this happy. It was hard for Malcolm to keep up with Tulip, who was shaking her butt, and her feet had some crazy moves. Malcolm grabbed hold and said to Tulip, "Hey, slow down, baby girl! We got all night!"

Tulip looked up at Malcolm and threw her head back and laughed. They continued to dance.

Tulip was enjoying the night. She never knew that dancing could be so much fun. She fanned her face with her hands and looked around the room. There were young and old colored folks of all different skin tones, just like Misses Chiles had said. Tulip looked around the room for Malcolm when suddenly, someone grabbed her wrist and spun her around.

"Hey, pretty girl," said Jessie. "Did that man of yours leave you all alone?"

Tulip smiled.

"Oh, I got a smile. Come on, let's show these folks how to cut a rug."

With that, Tulip and Jessie were in the middle of the dance floor. Folks began to clap and holler, "Go, Go, Go!" Tulip was having fun and laughed out loud. Jessie laughed and spun around harder. *Boy,* he thought, *that Malcolm is a lucky fellow.*

Malcolm stood and watched Tulip. The liquor slid smoothly down his throat, with a hint of heat.

As the night moved on, more drinks were had, and the music got slower. Tulip and Malcolm danced slow and close. Tulip loved the slow dancing, and being held by Malcolm. She felt so happy, and thought about how her life had taken a wonderful turn. Tulip prayed that she would always be in Malcolm's arms. She knew then that she would love him forever. They kissed and held each other close, moving to the music as one.

Promises made in the night sometimes do not see the daylight;
The heart takes a chance and hope that it gets it right;
Like rain in spring and sun in the summer,
one's expectation of love is not just dust in the wind
that blows away freely before it begins;
It's more like air below water that's engulfs
your air with joy and the hope for more.

chapter twenty-two

Falling in Love

*A*s Tulip and Malcolm ground their bodies together, sweat soaked through their clothes, and their eyes locked. Their lips connected, sending thunderbolts to their groins. Tulip could hardly contain herself as Malcolm's strong hands gently caressed and stroked her buttocks. She moved further into his body. She felt the stiffness of his manhood as it pressed against her Secret through her sweat-soaked dress. If not for shame, Tulip would have undressed and given herself freely to Malcolm right on the dance floor. Tulip and Malcolm were caught in desire as they swayed to the music.

Malcolm slowly raised his head and called Tulip's name in a husky voice. "Hey, baby girl," he said softly.

"Yes," Tulip said, as if she was in a dream. No worries, no pain, no sorrows. She wanted to stay here.

"We gotta be getting on," said Malcolm.

Not wanting to leave Malcolm's embrace, Tulip didn't answer, but she slowly backed away and gave him the most seductive smile he had ever seen. Hand-in-hand, they walked from the dance hall.

No words were spoken as they reached their buggy. Malcolm helped Tulip into the buggy and went to untie the horses. There were only a few buggies and wagons left in the field. Malcolm noticed in the distance that the dance hall had darkened. There was a chill in the air, but Malcolm still felt the heat from Tulip's body. He jumped on the buggy and called out to the horses to get moving.

Tulip rested her head on Malcolm's shoulder. She felt so happy and safe. She felt love.

As Malcolm pushed closer to home, Tulip hummed a soft song. *So she sings,* thought Malcolm.

Feeling silly, Tulip stopped. She had been humming a song she had heard in the dance hall:

> *Take me to heaven, touch me with your eyes,*
> *make my night yours, give me, sweet baby,*
> *what my body yearns for.*
> *You touch me spiritually, you got that black magic,*
> *when you touch me.*
> *Can't get enough, give me more, more, more...*

"No, don't stop singing. You have a beautiful voice," Malcolm said as he looked at Tulip's beautiful face in the darkness of the night.

"I've hit the jackpot!" Malcolm shouted so loud that animals in the woods scurried in fear of the human voice. "Not only was she the prettiest little sweet thing at the party, but she was the best dancer, and now, she can sing like a bird!

"I think I'll make this girl right here my wife!" Malcolm shouted loudly.

With that announcement, Tulip sat straight up from resting her head on Malcolm's shoulder. "Malcolm, did you have too much to drink? Surely, you don't want *me* for your wife?" Tulip asked, afraid that Malcolm was just drunk, or caught up in the passion of the night.

Malcolm drew the horses to a stop and turned to face Tulip. He could barely make out her face in the darkness of the night, but her features were etched in his mind. No light was needed. Malcolm lifted his hand and stroked Tulip's thick, full, long and coarse hair, which was damp with sweat from heavy dancing. Hearing sniffling, Malcolm withdrew his hand from her hair and touched her face. Tulip's face was wet with tears. Malcolm became worried. "Tulip, why are you crying? I'm sorry if I offended you."

Tulip answered with a shaking voice, "Malcolm, you want me to be your wife, but I'm nothing. I have nothing, and I am not ever going to be nothing," she cried through tears.

"*Nothing?*" Malcolm yelled passionately. "Tulip, don't you know that you are a beautiful woman and I love you? Don't ever say that you're nothing, because you're everything to me."

Tulip was speechless. She lay her head back on Malcolm's shoulder and they proceeded home to their new life. Tulip felt like she was laying on a bed of flowers, and the sweet scent of lilies and roses engulfed her senses. Her body was tingling with desire.

She opened her eyes to Malcolm standing before her. How strong and muscular was his smooth, brown body! Malcolm was a beautiful man, her man. His manhood was fully exposed and it was long, black, hard, and dripping with desire. Tulip's legs slowly opened wide as Malcolm mounted her, looking directly into her eyes, which were highlighted by the glow the night's full moon. They had separate hay beds in the loft, but tonight, they would share one. Even the farm animals sensed the aroma of lovemaking. Together, their bodies moved as one.

Malcolm slowly kissed Tulip's small, perky breasts. Malcolm thought that Tulip's breasts seemed fuller and bigger than before. He attributed it to good eating. The girl had become a woman right before his eyes. This was his woman and his future wife. Pushing that thought aside, Malcolm focused on not releasing too soon. He wanted to enjoy this time and pleasure his woman.

Tulip's body was wet with excitement. She and Malcolm had been intimate before, but for some reason, this time was different. Her body was pulling him in deeper, and she groaned and moved in rhythm with him. Tulip had never had an orgasm, so she didn't know what was happening when the feeling of pure passion rushed through her body. "Oh my God!"

Malcolm quickly covered Tulip's mouth so that her moans wouldn't scare the animals. "It's okay, Malcolm," she said breathlessly, still trying to calm herself.

With only a pulsating energy between them, she reached up to cover Malcolm's mouth as he yelled out, "Oh my God!"

"Malcolm! You up, boy?" called out Mister Chiles. "It's time to get to moving, son," It was quiet in the barn. Mister Chiles looked up the ladder toward the loft. He didn't want to intrude on Tulip and Malcolm's privacy.

"Malcolm!" called out Mister Chiles. Thinking he was dreaming, Malcolm sat straight up and tried to focus. His head was spinning from the liquor, dancing, and loving.

Yea! He thought as he looked down at his sleeping beauty. *Maybe I could get just a quick little more.* Malcolm let his hand stroke Tulip's big, round, pretty buttocks.

"Malcolm! Son, are you coming?" yelled Mister Chiles.

"I'm up! I'm coming sir," said Malcolm hurriedly, embarrassed that he hadn't realized that Mister Chiles was in the barn. Malcolm jumped up and slipped into his work clothes. "Be right with you, Mister Chiles!"

"Okay, I'll be waiting in the wagon. Make it fast, we got make up for lost time," said Mister Chiles with a grin on his face.

When Malcolm jumped in the wagon with Mister Chiles, he was still trying to gather himself. Mister Chiles just grinned and told the horses to get to moving.

Tulip turned over and reached out her hand to touch Malcolm, but the space was empty. Tulip called out, "Malcolm, Malcolm!" Receiving no answer, she laid back down on the makeshift hay bed, but suddenly, she noticed the flower lying beside her. It was a single lily, just like the one Malcolm had given her before the dance. She smiled, fell back, and kicked up her feet with joy.

Tulip realized that she did not have her nightdress on, and was naked as the day she was born. Tulip pulled up the blanket to cover her nakedness and smiled. In fact, she laughed out loud, and laughed, and laughed. "He asked me to be his wife," Tulip said to herself with a smile.

Tulip helped Misses Chiles and the children in the fields picking vegetables for supper. Tulip knew she was late for chores and was embarrassed. "Sorry," she said as she approached Misses Chiles. "I didn't mean to oversleep." Tulip kneeled down in the dirt to pull up some potatoes.

"No need to apologize," said Misses Chiles. "I hope you and Malcolm had a good time. You're young, and you worked hard for your keep, so no harm in a little fun and rest," she said, smiling. "And I want to hear about your night. I heard some noise coming from the barn in night, just assumed it was you and Malcolm arriving."

Tulip felt embarrassed again. She lowered her eyes from Misses Chiles's gaze and began pulling potatoes with no response.

Misses Chiles smiled and thought, *Young love—a beautiful thing!*

Tulip worked hard pulling and digging up potatoes. She didn't feel the heat or even mind the hard work. Her mind was caught up in the dance and lovemaking from the night before—and, more importantly, Malcolm had asked her to be his wife. She couldn't wait until Malcolm came home. Tulip hoped he would remember, and hadn't changed his mind. *Suppose he didn't remember*, Tulip fretted. *Oh Mama, let him still want me for his wife. I so love him.*

The day seemed long, but Tulip didn't mind. She was caught up in her thoughts and was even humming a little song. When the evening approached and the sun was setting, Malcolm and Mister Chiles arrived home. Malcolm wanted to rush into the barn and take Tulip in his arms. His head was clear, and he remembered everything from the night before. He hoped that Tulip still wanted to be his wife someday, just not right now. First, they needed to make plans and save some money for a place of their own. It wasn't that Malcolm didn't want to marry Tulip, just that he had make sure that he could take care of a wife and family. He and Tulip would talk after supper.

Malcolm could see Tulip coming toward him—beads of sweat on her forehead, headscarf, dirt, and all, but she was still a pretty sight for his eyes, and his heart was happy.

Seeing Malcolm in the distance, Tulip hesitated a little. Her heart skipped a beat with a flutter of nervousness. She hadn't expected him so soon. Tulip wanted to clean up a bit before he saw her. She used the bottom of her apron to wipe some of the sweat and dirt from her face and hands. She didn't want Malcolm to see her all sweaty and dirty, but that was not to be, as Malcolm was already walking her way.

"Hey there, baby girl!" yelled out Malcolm, with a big grin on his face. Tulip slowly approached him and then took off running in his direction. Malcolm started a slow run toward her.

Misses Chiles, the children, and Mister Chiles just stood there, watching. As Tulip and Malcolm got closer to each other, they both stopped in their tracks.

"Hey there," said Malcolm trying to catch his breath.

"Hey," said Tulip breathless.

My, My, so sweet is our love,
It takes us to the highest and bring us from the lowest,
No pretend, not fake, so real,
All this right here is ours.
Don't leave it waiting and wanting, move it forward
Our love is here for taking.
Only our love could bring us together in this time and place.

chapter twenty-three

Asking Questions

*L*ife on the Chiles's farm moved at a slow pace. Several months had gone by since the dance and Malcolm asking Tulip to be his wife. Tulip was ready to marry Malcolm the next day, but she and Malcolm had agreed to wait until they had saved money for their own home. Malcolm was working harder and taking on more jobs to save money so that he and Tulip could marry and start their own family. They were even very careful with their lovemaking. They didn't want a family to come too soon.

Tulip missed him when he was gone so frequently. She spent a lot of time in the house with Misses Chiles and the children, and she and Faith had become good friends.

One evening, after completing their chores, Tulip and Faith walked down to the river for a relaxing time. Malcolm was away, and Misses Chiles was busy with the younger children. As Tulip and Faith walked along the banks of the river, Tulip told Faith about how she had been afraid to cross the bridge when they first arrived, and how Malcolm had helped her. Faith laughed aloud as Tulip described how she almost fell into the raging river.

"You don't swim a lick?" asked Faith.

"Not a lick," Tulip replied. "And, I don't want to," she announced, with indignation.

"That's silly," said Faith. "Mama said God made the river for us to cleanse our body, drink and nourish the land." Faith looked to the heavens. "The river and water are gifts from God."

"Well, that's good and fine, but you won't catch me thrashing about in all that water. Damn near killed myself," Tulip said, shaking her head.

"Oh Tulip, that's why I love you: you are so stubborn."

Both girls laughed.

They rested by the riverbank and looked at the blue sky and clouds that resembled big, white balls of cotton. There was a gentle breeze flowing through the air, and the river made a rustling noise as if it was singing. Birds flew over their heads and the animals of the forest called out to each other.

"Faith?" said Tulip.

"Yes?" Faith replied.

"Can I ask you a very serious question?"

"Yes, but only if I can ask you one," replied Faith.

"Yes, anything," said Tulip. She continued, "How did Mister Chiles—I mean, your Papa—come to marry your Mama?

"They were in school together and fell in love," Faith replied.

"But whites and colored don't go to school together," Tulip responded, questioningly.

"I know that, silly," said Faith.

"So how could they meet in school," persisted Tulip, "with your Mama being white and your Papa being colored?"

"Oh my goodness, Tulip, have you gone straight crazy? Mama is just as colored as you, Malcolm, and me for all account. Mama said that colored folks are like flowers and come in all shades of color," Faith continued. "Mama says when she born, her Mama had to give her away because she was white and had a colored child. Her family didn't want nothing to do with her. Mama was sent to live with a sharecropper family. They raised her as one of theirs, but they told her the truth about her real family. So that's how she met my Papa: at the colored school."

Tulip was speechless. All this time, she and Malcolm thought that Misses Chiles was white, and she was colored, just like them. *My, my,* thought Tulip.

"I answered your question," said Faith. "Now I have one for you."

"Okay," said Tulip, wondering about the question to come. "What is it?"

"I know you and Malcolm plan to marry, and you sleep separately in the loft, like brother and sister, but I was wondering…" Faith hesitated.

"What is it? Come out with it," Tulip said, getting a little frustrated and sensing where this conversation was headed.

"God sakes, give me a minute." Faith continued, "Have you did it with Malcolm?" It came out of Faith's mouth so fast that Tulip didn't understand the question.

"*Did what, Faith?*" she yelled as she stood brushing the wood chips and dirt from her skirt.

"I'm sorry, I didn't mean to upset you," said Faith, "but I overheard Mama saying to Papa that you were looking a little plump around the hips and breasts and she hoped that wasn't in the family way, given that you and Malcolm aren't man and wife." Faith lowered her head, sensing that she had offended her friend.

Tulip was stunned and speechless. She knew that she had gained weight since arriving at the Chiles's farm, but that was to be expected, given Misses Chiles's good cooking and plenty of food to eat. Tulip wasn't concerned that the monthly bleeding had stopped. In fact, she had been glad. Since the night of the dance, her and Malcolm had made love every chance they could. She loved giving herself to Malcolm. But it was not to be shared with anyone else, let alone her friend Faith, who was still a little girl.

"*No!*" Tulip replied hastily. "No, it's a sin to be with a man that's not your husband."

"I know, I know, Tulip," said Faith, relieved that Tulip was still speaking to her.

"Come," Tulip said. "It's time to head back, and Misses Chiles may worry."

Faith did not respond. She was ashamed that she had asked such a question, but she was still curious, and longed to be kissed by someone.

Lying in the loft, Tulip was deep in thought. She wondered, *How would I know if I was with child?* Tulip had noticed the changes in her body, such as the fullness of her breasts and her nipples, which had become big and sensitive. *I'll be seventeen in a month, so maybe this is what happens at seventeen.* But she couldn't deny that her appetite had changed drastically. She was always hungry, and sometimes, would sneak something to eat when Malcolm was asleep. Also, her belly was getting bigger and harder, but all the layers of clothing hid it.

Tulip thought and paced. Tears streamed down fast. *I don't want to go to hell!* Tulip's Mama had told her that it was sin to let someone touch her Secret other than her husband. While she loved Malcolm, it was still a sin. What if she was with child? Tulip panicked. The sheer thought sent lightning bolts up her spine. Malcolm made it very clear that there should be no children until after they were married.

Tulip was exhausted when Malcolm arrived home. She had been

crying and was in a fit. She couldn't even summon her Mama or the field of lilies.

"Hey there, what are you doing up here all alone?" asked Malcolm.

Tulip looked up through tear-filled red eyes at the man that she loved more than life and blurted out, "Let's not wait. I want to be your wife *now!*"

Malcolm looked down at this beautiful girl—woman—of his and said with a big grin, "I don't understand the rush, but sure." He smiled. They kissed.

So here we go becoming one together,
forever we say in the passion of love,
Who's to say that this wasn't meant to be,
me with him and him with me,
Time will tell if the love will prevail, but each will give it all to
ensure that it's more than just a fairy tale…

chapter twenty-four

Happily Ever After

"Tulip, stop all that fidgeting." Misses Chiles swore as she struggled to pin Tulip's wedding dress. "You're getting thicker by the day. The wedding is tomorrow, and I got to make more adjustments to this dress." Misses Chiles shook her head in despair.

"I'm sorry to be so much trouble, ma'am," Tulip said, lowering her head.

"Oh, nonsense, girl, and stop 'ma'aming' me. Makes me feel old."

Misses Chiles stood to face Tulip. "Now, I have been meaning to talk with you, but now is not the time, with the wedding and all, but your weight gain, as well as other woman matters, have not gone unnoticed, and are means for concern—not a bad concern, if you know what I mean."

"Ma'am—I mean Misses Chiles—I think I know what you mean" Tulip said in a very small voice.

Misses Chiles hugged Tulip and rubbed her back, saying, "It's going to be alright, baby girl."

Mister Chiles and Misses Chiles had spread the news about Tulip and Malcolm's wedding around the town. Many folks had come to know Malcolm from the jobs he took on and thought him to be a fine young man. Quite a few of the young girls and even women from the neighboring farms were smitten with Malcolm, but he had let them know quickly that he was spoken for. The men that Malcolm came to know encouraged him to have fun with the ladies before he settled down with a wife and bunch of knappy-headed children, but Malcolm just laughed them off. Folks were happy to come to the wedding, but mostly, they just wanted some good food and drink, and to talk and dance. Living was about work and fun.

The Chiles children were excited about the wedding, especially Faith. While they didn't really understand, they knew that it was going to be fun and that they would get to wear their nice clothes and shoes. But Faith had her own reason to be excited. Mama had made her a pretty new dress, almost like the one Malcolm bought for Tulip to wear to their dance. Misses Chiles copied the design perfectly. Faith thought about how pretty she would look, and she secretly hoped that Ben would think so, too. Faith twirled around and around.

"Faith!" Misses Chiles yelled. "Why are you wasting time dancing around?"

"Sorry, Mama," Faith said sheepishly.

"Go on and get the water heated up for your sisters' bath. Folks will be here soon, and I have to finish the cooking and help Tulip. Now, be quick about it, there is no time to waste." Misses Chiles waved Faith along.

Tulip slipped on her wedding dress, which was made of white satin and lace. The gown fit her body like a glove and accented every curve. Misses Chiles had taken her time and hand-sewn round white buttons to look like pearls. While it was a simple dress, it was the perfect dress, and made Tulip grin from ear to ear. Tulip wore a lace veil that Misses Chiles found in town at the local store. It was really a dolly for a tabletop, but it made the perfect veil.

As Misses Chiles buttoned the dress, she was glad that she had opened the waist a little, because Tulip was mighty thick in the middle and the top. Her breasts were sitting up, full, round and high. *But, that's for another day. We just got get these two married,* thought Misses Chiles.

"There. All done," she announced, as she turned Tulip around to face the mirror.

Tulip couldn't believe her eyes. She was absolutely beautiful. *Who was this woman before her eyes?* Misses Chiles had pinned up Tulip's hair and adorned it with lilies. A touch of rouge was added to her cheeks, and a little on her lips.

Tulip's thoughts immediately went to her Mama. She felt her presence all around. Her mind slowly drifted to the field of lilies, and she was engulfed in the sweet aroma of the flowers—flowers of every color and type. Tulip touched the flowers as she walked along.

"Mama, Mama!" Tulip called out. "Where are you? Today is my wedding day: I am going to be married!" she said to the air. "Mama, I want you to see me. I'm beautiful."

I'm here, my baby girl, and yes, I see you and you are beautiful, Mama said, smiling as she and Tulip embraced.

Folks had arrived and gathered around the yard. The young pastor and Malcolm stood under a tree and watched Tulip and Mister Chiles approach.

Malcolm was looking smart and handsome as ever in his new pants, shoes, and white shirt. His hair was slicked back and shining in the sunlight. Sweat was rolling down Malcolm's face from standing in the heat, as well as the anticipation of becoming a husband. Malcolm thought that he wasn't ready to be a husband, but Tulip was insistent, and didn't want to be intimate anymore until they married, so he didn't see any reason to wait. Nor did he feel that he had a choice in the matter. But he wasn't ready to be a Papa, that's for sure.

Malcolm smiled toward Tulip, who was as pretty as the stars at night. Their guests whooped, hooted, and marveled at how beautiful she looked. Many of the younger girls simply looked Tulip up and down and rolled their eyes with envy, however, which didn't go unnoticed by Tulip.

"By the grace of our Lord Savior, and the authority vested in me by the state of New York, I now pronounce you man and wife. What God has brought together, let no man tear apart," the preacher announced in a loud and thundering voice.

"Go head, boy, kiss your beautiful bride," the preacher urged Malcolm.

Overcome with nerves, Malcolm timidly lifted Tulip's veil and gently placed a peck on her lips. In that precious moment, their eyes met and locked, and there was neither a sound, nor any movement. It was like the earth stood still, and they were the only two people in the world. There was a quiet rustling of leaves.

Malcolm looked at his young wife and said, "Hey girl."

Tulip looked at her husband and said, "Hey boy."

The food, drink, and dance went on until dusk. Tulip and Malcolm laughed and hugged and kissed each other, and many other folks. Even the envious girls told Tulip that she was lucky to marry Malcolm, and that she looked nice.

Mister Chiles and Misses Chiles danced together and kissed. The children danced. Tulip noticed that Faith had disappeared for a while, but she soon reappeared, looking red in the face and smiling.

Mister Chiles asked everyone to settle down and follow him, including the bride and groom. Tulip and Malcolm looked confused.

They didn't know what to think, but his house, his rules, so everyone trotted along down a long path behind the house.

After a short walk, there it stood: a little cabin. It was not much, just a one-room structure with a couple of front windows. Mister Chiles looked at his wife and smiled, and then turned to Tulip and Malcolm and said, "Malcolm, since the day you and Tulip stumbled upon my land, you both have proven to be fine, upstanding people. You two have become the Misses' and mine's children.

"We make this promise on your wedding day to always look out and protect you, as well as your children. Now this here cabin isn't much, but we own it free and clear, including the land that surrounds it. Son and Daughter, please always know what we have is yours. So, with that said, the Misses and I prepared this little cabin for you two to start your new life and family. No more sleeping in the barn like a hired hand."

It was quiet and there wasn't a dry eye in the bunch, except for some of the menfolk. Finally, someone gave out a big whoop. With that, everyone cheered.

The folks began to look around the small cabin. They knew the value of having a roof over your head and a place to call home. Some of the menfolk patted Mister Chiles on the back. Womenfolk nodded and smiled at Misses Chiles. The Chiles children all clapped because they had helped to clean the cabin and knew about the gift. Tulip and Malcolm were speechless. They looked at each other and said in unison, "Our home!"

As night fell, folks began to say their goodbyes and make their way home. They were full of drink and good food, and were exhausted from dancing. But the next day, they would rise early and come together, as work would not wait.

Together, Misses Chiles, Mister Chiles, Malcolm, Tulip, and

Faith said their goodbyes, hugged, and gave thanks. Faith slyly smiled at Ben, but it didn't go unnoticed by her Mama and Papa. The younger children had long been asleep. Everyone was ready to leave, and the happy couple wanted to start their night.

Tulip and Malcolm turned to Mister and Misses Chiles. Malcolm stepped forward and bowed his head.

"Sir, ma'am, Tulip and me want you to know that we will never forget this day and your kindness. Since losing our parents and our struggles, God found a way to lead us to you, and for that, we are eternally grateful. Know that we will repay you one day for your kindness. This wedding was more than we could have ever imagined.

"The cabin, the cabin…" started Malcolm, as Tulip looked on, crying.

"Enough already," said Mister Chiles. "We got plenty of time for your thank yous. This is your most sacred night, your wedding night. Now go!" Mister Chiles said, pushing Malcolm toward his new home.

"Okay! But know, sir, I will be up first thing in the morning ready to work." Malcolm said proudly.

"No, you won't! No work for you or Tulip tomorrow. It's your honeymoon," said Mister Chiles, with a wink.

"Thank you, sir," Malcolm said, blushing. "Tulip and me will just grab a few—" Malcolm stopped mid-sentence, just realizing that Tulip, Misses Chiles, and Faith had left. Malcolm was so caught up in emotion that he hadn't seen Tulip leave.

"Son, go! Your wife is waiting," Mister Chiles said lovingly.

"Okay, but I'll just grab a few things from the barn."

"Boy, if you don't get your hide home, I'll carry you myself!" Mister Chiles said with force.

Knowing Mister Chiles was serious this time, Malcolm took off running toward his new home, grinning all the way to his new wife and life.

As Malcolm approached the cabin, he could see a light twinkling from the window, and smoke rising from the chimney.

What? How? Who? thought Malcolm. As he pushed the cabin door, a warmth engulfed his head. There was a fire burning, its smoke rising through the chimney, and candles were lit throughout the room. A bottle of drink and two glasses were placed on the table, along with fruit, sweet bread, jam, and cheese. Lilies were scattered about the cabin's wood floor.

As Malcolm looked around, his eyes stopped: before him was an angel. Tulip appeared, dressed in a pretty white nightdress, with her hair cascading down her breast. She stood by a bed with cast iron railings and a footboard, embroidered pillows, and a beautiful quilt.

Tulip said, "I hope that you remember the quilt. I saved it from your wagon. I didn't steal it. It was just too beautiful to leave in the woods. I hope you don't mind."

Malcolm was overcome with emotion and choked back tears. Quietly, Malcolm said, "It was my Maw's. One of her prized possessions. Thank you for saving it." Malcolm walked up to Tulip and looked into her eyes.

"Misses Thornton, I promise to love you, protect you, and provide for you. I make this promise to you before God, because it was Him who brought you to me on that fateful road." They embraced and kissed. Malcolm let his hands roam the fullness of Tulip's buttocks, and his mind and manhood quickly registered the roundness and softness.

Tulip moaned with pleasure. She and Malcolm had waited months without loving for this special night.

Malcolm slowly reached down and lifted Tulip's nightdress.

"Wait," said Tulip, "I need to blow out candles and turn down the lamp."

"No," protested Malcolm. "I want to see you. No more hiding in the dark. I want to see my beautiful wife, all of you."

Tulip lifted her arms and Malcolm proceeded to lift her nightdress over her head. He let his eyes soak up her beautiful, thick brown body. Malcolm thought she had really matured for a girl of seventeen. His Nature rose.

Feeling embarrassed under Malcolm's gaze and thinking that he found her fat and ugly, Tulip tried to cover her body with her hands.

"Stop," said Malcolm. "You are my wife and you are beautiful. I've watched you hide your body and fight your demons at night," he confessed, "but you are safe now, and I will not let anything or anyone hurt you, ever."

Tears streamed down Tulip's face.

Tell him. Tell him, a voice within her urged. *Tell him.*

"Malcolm, there is something that I must tell you," whispered Tulip.

"Quiet, Tulip, now is not the time for talking, only loving, and girl, I want to love you right tonight." Malcolm lowered Tulip onto their first bed.

Tulip, now losing her nerve, was also hot with passion. Her stomach rose up and down, her big black nipples stood up with full attention, her heart raced, beams of sweat formed on forehead, and wetness ran down her thighs from her Secret.

Malcolm could no longer contain himself. He kissed his wife's forehead, both of her eyes, her nose, and gently on her lips. He kissed each ear lobe, her neck, and moved down to her nipples. Malcolm sucked each one gently, while Tulip moved and moaned under him.

Tulip stroked her husband's back and kissed his neck as he

slowly moved from her breast to her stomach. Tulip, caught up in the rapture, didn't realize what was happening until her Secret exploded with fire from Malcolm's tongue. Tulip sat straight up, as her thighs locked onto Malcolm head.

"Malcolm, no, no," she tried to say breathlessly. "Please, no. Stop, Malcolm," she pleaded in passion.

Malcolm stopped, looked up at Tulip, and said, "I will stop if you tell me you don't like it." Tulip eased back down and opened her legs wider.

Two became one, embodied in a web of life and at this time,
no desire of flight;
The passion is real, and all is given, nothing is taken;
only love not to be undone;
We speak as we, there is no individual,
just a fleeing thought to be free;
Yet so thankful, so blessed to share moment by
moment in the same space;
Together we commit to each other,
not to part from another, so we pray.

chapter twenty-five

Seeing Ghosts

*A*s the months went by, Tulip and Malcolm settled into their routine of becoming a family. They worked hard at the Chiles's farm to repay their debt, and Malcolm often went into town to seek work at other farms. He was a hard worker, and many nights, he could not make it home to Tulip.

Those nights were hard for Tulip, so she would ask Faith to keep her company after supper. Most of the time, Tulip would fall asleep on Faith. Tulip was tired all the time, and sleeping was not always pleasant: many nights, Tulip would scream out loud, sometimes for her Mama, never for her Papa. Sometimes she just cried, and Malcolm thought it was best to leave it be, but he was still worried.

On some occasions, Tulip would accompany Malcolm into town. It was a long ride, but Tulip loved seeing the shops and people moving about. She also got to spend more time with Malcolm. When Mister Chiles had other work to do, he would send Malcolm to town for supplies or to pick up things that Mister Chiles had ordered. Misses Chiles would also have them pick up materials that she used to make clothes for the family. She was a very good seamstress and other folks had started asking her to make items for them.

Folks were a little more comfortable with Misses Chiles since Tulip and Malcolm's wedding. Like Tulip, many people thought that Misses Chiles was a white woman, and they didn't want any trouble. Other folks knew her story, and about the family that raised her.

"Tulip, go to the general store and pick up Misses Chiles's order while I tend to Mister Chiles's supplies and horses. The order is already settled. Just let them know Misses Chiles sent you for pick-up," said Malcolm. "Meet me back at the wagon when you're done. If I ain't here, just wait, and don't go wandering off daydreaming like before." He pointed a playful finger in Tulip's direction.

"I ain't no child, Malcolm," Tulip said as she stepped down from the wagon.

"I know that! I just want you to be careful, so don't nobody get no ideas."

Tulip understood his concern. There were always a lot of menfolk moving about in the town, and sometimes, they would make little comments and eye her backside. Their stares made her uncomfortable.

The bells above the door chimed as Tulip entered the store.

"Good Morning, ma'am," Tulip said politely as she approached the older white woman behind the counter in the store. The store was the only one in town that sold women's clothing, including hats, undergarments, fabric, and just about anything else a seamstress would need. But most importantly, it was where a person could order from the Sears, Roebuck Catalog. Orders would be delivered directly to the store, where they could pick them up and pay for them.

"I am here to pick up Misses Chiles' order." Tulip spoke just above a whisper.

"Sorry, gal, but you got to speak up. I never seen you before. Are you from around here?" inquired the white woman.

"Yes ma'am," said Tulip.

"The colored fellow—I believe his name is Malcolm—usually picks up the Chiles's order," said the white woman with suspicion.

"I know, ma'am. I'm with Malcolm. Misses Chiles asked me to pick up her order because Malcolm has to get Mister Chiles supplies."

"Are you alright, child?"

"Yes, Ma'am, just a little warm from the heat," replied Tulip, sweat dripping on her forehead.

"Well, sat over there. Don't want you falling down in the store, making a mess of things. It'll take me a minute or so to get your package. Don't go touching nothing because I know your kind. I'll know if something is missing."

"Yes Ma'am," muttered Tulip.

The woman walked to the back of the store behind a makeshift curtain. Tulip sat in the chair with her hands folded and her eyes straight ahead, too scared to look at anything. As she sat, the bells above the store door rang, signaling that someone had entered.

Tulip heard the walking. The steps were loud. She was too afraid to look up.

"Hello? Is anyone working here? *Where the hell are you?*" shouted the man angrily. "For Christ's sake, I don't got all day, dammit!"

"Hold your horses!" the white woman yelled from behind the curtain. "I'll be right there in a minute," she said.

"Well, make it quick! I don't have all day," shouted the man as he began to slowly move around the store, commenting on different items.

Tulip could feel the man's eyes on her, and he seemed to be moving in her direction. She dared not look up. She was sweating even harder. The man started to whistle and hum. Deep in Tulip's body, the whistle sounded familiar. It awakened something in her soul that sent chills through her spine.

"Well, finally!" said the man.

"I told you a minute, and it was a minute," said the white woman. "I had to find an order, so let me take care of this first and I will be right with you, Mister Betts," replied the white woman.

Tulip's heart pounded so loud she thought it was going to jump out of her skin. Sweat dripped down her face and her hands trembled. Warm urine leaked from between her legs, seeped down her thighs, and rested on the floor. Her hairs stood on edge as she replayed what she had heard only seconds before. *Did she say Betts? I've heard that name before. But where?*

"Well, looka here, Catherine, I'm not gonna sit here while you wait on some n—r girl," announced Papa Betts. "My wife got a package delivered, so get it so I can be on my way."

The white woman and Papa Betts stared at each other for a few moments before she slammed Tulip's package on the counter and walked to the back without uttering a word.

"Stupid bitch," mumbled Papa Betts as he looked in Tulip's direction, eyeing her up and down with lust.

Tulip was about to suffocate under his stare. She could neither move nor take her eyes off the floor. She felt nausea rise up in her throat and knew she'd better run out before she spilled out on the white woman's floor, but her legs wouldn't move. The recognition of Papa Betts hit her with such force that it made her head spin. "It can't be!" she yelled aloud, rocking back and forth.

"What the hell's wrong with you, n—r?" yelled Papa Betts.

"What's all the ruckus out here?" said the white woman.

Tulip jumped and staggered out the door. As soon as the fresh air hit her face, she took off running.

Tulip ran past the wagon where Malcolm was loading the

supplies. Confused, he stopped what he was doing started running after her. People moved out her way, thinking that she was having some type of fit. The white woman stepped out of the store and yelled to Tulip that she had forgotten the package.

Malcolm ran as fast as he could, wondering what was going on, and if someone had hurt her.

"Tulip! Tulip!" He called out. "*Tulip, please stop!*" Malcolm called out as he ran to her.

The townspeople all stopped to look at the two colored folk running through the square. Women grabbed their children in fear that they would get hurt. Tulip's hair swung wildly as she ran with her arms thrashing about. She didn't hear Malcolm call out. Her mind was somewhere else in time. Tears streamed down her face. She ran as fast she could until she collapsed right in the middle of the dirt road.

The town's only doctor, a white man, witnessed all the commotion. Seeing Tulip passed out in the road, he ran to help. Malcolm was kneeling and holding Tulip in his arms, calling her name. The doctor told Malcolm that they needed to get her inside. Along with a few other colored men (no other white man would help) the doctor helped Malcolm bring Tulip into his office.

It wasn't customary for the doctor to service coloreds, but on occasion, and for the right price, he did. He also knew Malcolm from the Chiles's farm and the Chileses were good people.

"What's wrong with her, Dr. Foster?" Malcolm asked with a distraught face. "I'll pay you, just tell me what's wrong with my wife," Malcolm pleaded. He could not lose his precious Tulip, his family.

"We were only apart for a few minutes. Did someone hurt her, doctor?"

Dr. Foster replied calmly, "Malcolm, take a seat over there and I will let you know something as soon as I check out your wife. Please sit down, son," said Dr. Foster as he closed the door to his examination room.

Malcolm did not sit down, and paced up and down the quiet hallway. He noticed that a group of onlookers had gathered outside of the doctor's office, some peering through the glass. Malcolm didn't care. His only concern was his wife.

Finally, Dr. Foster came out of the examination room. Malcolm stopped pacing and approached the doctor. His heart was pumping fast and the palms of his hands were sweating.

"It's nothing serious. In fact, some women are subject to fits when they're expecting," laughed Dr. Foster.

"'Expecting?' Expecting what?" Malcolm was puzzled.

"A baby! What'd you think? A horse?" asked Dr. Foster, giggling.

"*Baby?*" said Malcolm as he looked at Doctor Foster.

"Yes, you're going to be a Papa. I would say any day now! I believe the heat got to her. Get her home, let her rest, and in the next couple days, I will send the colored midwife to assist Misses Chiles with the delivery.

"I've given your wife something to calm her down. I'll get some fellas to help you put her in the back of the wagon, so she can rest. Don't worry, she will be fine," Dr. Foster said as he walked away.

Tulip slept all the way home. She moaned and yelled out a few times, but mostly, she just slept. Malcolm's mind was racing a mile a minute. He wasn't ready to be a Papa, and thought that he and Tulip had been careful. *Why didn't she tell him?* he wondered. *How could the baby be ready so fast? What about their plans to move on from the Chileses? How would he ever pay off his debt to the them with a baby coming?*

Within three days of Tulip collapsing in town, Misses Chiles sent word to Dr. Foster for the colored mid-wife. She was not surprised about the arrival of the baby: she knew before Tulip and Malcolm's wedding that Tulip was with child. That's why she was pleased when they decided to get married.

Misses Chiles knew that Tulip didn't understand what was happening to her body, and when she tried to approach the matter with Tulip, Tulip would change the subject, or rush off. Misses Chiles knew that Malcolm didn't know about the baby, either. Men were always clueless about pregnancy, right up until the baby is right before their eyes, like a miracle that they had nothing to do with.

Misses Chiles smiled to herself. It was going to be okay. Malcolm was good man, and Tulip would make a good mother. Misses Chiles just hoped the midwife made it soon, because Tulip had already started the birthing process. Misses Chiles knew how to birth a baby, given the number of babies she had had herself, but she would need help, and Faith could only do so much, daydreaming all the time.

Eventually, the colored midwife arrived. "Girl," she said as calmly as possible, "I'm going to need you get those legs open wide as possible, so your baby can get some air." The midwife had birthed many babies in her time, and this time was no different. She knew that she needed to get that baby out quick, before it wouldn't be no baby.

"Girl, when I tell you to push, you push with all of the strength God gave you."

Tulip's mind was racing. She had not fully recovered from the events from town, and now this strange woman was all up in her private area telling her keep her legs wide open and push. Tulip was humiliated, laying fully naked with her legs wide open for the world to see. In a blur, she could see Misses Chiles wiping the sweat from her body, smiling down at her, and saying it would be okay. Faith was busy moving about like a scared rabbit with big, wide eyes. Tulip would not make eye contact.

Where is Malcolm? she wanted to yell out. *The pain in my back, my private area, it hurts so much,* she thought to herself.

"I need Malcolm!" she yelled.

"Push!" yelled the midwife, over and over. "Push! Harder, girl, so this baby can come out! *Push!*"

Tulip's last thought was, *Baby.*

"It's a girl!" exclaimed Misses Chiles, as she wiped the baby's body. "Tulip, you have a daughter and she is beautiful."

Washing her hands and sweat from her face, the colored midwife looked down at the newborn baby and thought to herself, *Yeah, she white. Seen that before, too!*

There is motion of the world,
the Gods of heaven set forth the next play;
You cannot stray, your actions will carry you,
because you have no say,
So let it flourish, guide your path,
let the heart create each beautiful way;
You created a stage, you are the star, give or take,
and direct what will come; do not fight,
Be guided; let rain of love shower down upon you,
for you are here; cherish each day!

chapter twenty-six

Solo

Misses Chiles gently placed the newborn on Tulip's breast. As she watched the baby seeking its mother's nipple, she was shocked by how much the baby reminded her of her own dear children when they were born: very white, with pink, peeling skin and fuzzy golden hair. But those light gray eyes with just a hint of blue were something else.

Misses Chiles just smiled and said, "Here, Tulip, your new beautiful daughter. I believe she's hungry and needs to be fed."

Misses Chiles pulled down the covering from Tulip's big brown breast and slowly guided Tulip's exhausted hands, one to her breast and the other to support her baby's head. Misses Chiles noticed that Tulip looked away and had not even glanced at her new daughter. She just followed Misses Chiles's commands as if she was in a trance. Both the midwife and Faith looked at Tulip strangely.

Misses Chiles massaged Tulip's breast so that the milk could flow. Tulip just stared toward the fire burning in the stove. Slowly, Misses Chiles guided the baby's mouth to Tulip's hard nipple, which was dripping with creamy, clear liquid. The baby latched on the nipple greedily.

Tulip gave a yell and just about threw the baby off her body. The baby let out a forceful cry.

As if she was just coming back to the world, Tulip finally looked at the pink, scaly thing that was demanding her breast.

"*Tulip!*" screamed Misses Chiles, which was the first time Tulip had ever heard Misses Chiles raise her voice. "Now, you behave yourself. This here is your daughter, and she needs to be fed," pleaded Misses Chiles. "I know you're scared, but look at her. She is so beautiful. Don't you want her to be nice and fed for when her Papa gets home?" Tulip looked up at Misses Chiles, and then down at her baby.

Tulip looked at her baby's hair, her face, ears, nose, hands, and feet. She pulled back the rough cloth that the baby was wrapped in. The baby kicked her feet. Her hands were moving, and she cried in protest. Tulip looked up at Misses Chiles with a confused look on her face, and asked, "Why is she white?"

"Don't be silly, Tulip! Some colored babies are born very light because we come in all colors. As time goes by, she will darken like you and Malcolm," Misses Chiles said lovingly. "Now, let's try one more time to get some of this milk in her before it dries."

The baby latched on to her Mama's hard, wet nipple, and sucked feverishly. Tulip grimaced in pain, but she didn't yell out. She looked down at this little thing sucking on her body and said to herself, "Who are you?"

As if hearing her, the baby opened her little eyes and looked up at Tulip's body. Their eyes connected. *Blue and gray eyes,* Tulip thought to herself. *Why?*

Misses Chiles went to take care of the midwife and told Faith to sit with Tulip. No words were exchanged between the two ladies as they walked back to the Chiles's main house. Both women were deep in thought, reliving their own experiences.

"Tulip," Faith said softly as she approached the makeshift bed.

"Your baby is so beautiful and tiny. I didn't know you were with child, but I did overhear Mama talking with Papa, thinking that you may be with child. What are you going to name her?" continued Faith. "She's so lovely like a little baby doll. Remember when I told you that Maw said we come in all colors? Your baby is just a different color from you and Malcolm, but she is still your baby."

Faith smiled. "You should name her like a princess, a name nobody else has."

Tulip smiled at Faith. She was such a good friend, and Tulip loved her like a sister. The baby had fallen asleep with Tulip's nipple still in her mouth. Tulip looked at the baby and took a deep breath. "I really didn't know I was with child," Tulip said, while looking down at the baby. "I knew I was getting fat, but I thought that was because I had plenty of food to eat. Malcolm and I wanted to wait to start a family until we were on our own. I was surprised when the white doctor in town told him that I was with child, and it would be coming soon."

"I don't know nothing about babies or being a mother," Tulip said, looking at Faith with sorrowful eyes.

"Oh, that's easy. Just take care of them like we do for the baby farm animals," Faith said with a laugh. "Don't worry, Tulip, I'll help you."

Faith gave Tulip a kiss, and then she kissed the baby's forehead. "But what will you name her?" she asked, anxiously.

Tulip looked around the cabin. She looked down at her sleeping baby. "I will call her Solo," said Tulip.

"It's a nice name, I guess, but why that name?" inquired Faith.

"Because she came into the world alone. Don't you see, Faith, I didn't know that I was even with child. She was alone in me, taking care of herself, with no Mama or Papa."

"Do you think Malcolm will like that name?" asked Faith.

"I don't care, that is what she will be called," Tulip said stubbornly.

Faith nodded and smiled, and said, "Solo it is. I will tell Mama, so that she can record it in the Bible."

Misses Chiles was standing on the porch when Mister Chiles and Malcolm came home. It had been a long day, and the sun was going down. She had checked in on Tulip and the baby, and all was going well. She gathered up the items leftover from her own babies to hold Tulip's baby over, at least until she could show Tulip how to make some new clothes. She also still had the cradle that each of the little ones slept in as a baby. Mister Chiles had made it with his own hands. Tulip could use it until the baby outgrew it.

Everything will be fine, she thought to herself. However, she was surprised when Faith told her what Tulip had named the baby and why. Misses Chiles's only reaction was, *Her baby, her choice.*

Misses Chiles watched as the two men walked the horses into the barn. While she was excited to share the news with Malcolm, she had her concerns, so she said a little prayer.

"Hey there!" she yelled as the two men walked from the barn.

Malcolm waved and turned to walk up the path toward his cabin.

"Malcolm!" called out Misses Chiles. Malcolm stopped as Misses Chiles walked toward him, and he noticed her big wide smile.

Malcolm thought to himself, *Well, that is a good sign.*

"Didn't want you to be concerned, but an unexpected visitor made their presence a little early," said Misses Chiles, grinning.

Malcolm wasn't quite comprehending what Misses Chiles was trying to say. "Does this have anything to do with Tulip?" questioned Malcolm. "Is she okay?"

Misses Chiles had to chuckle. "I swear, you men about as slow as they come. Just hurry on home, Malcolm—don't want to spoil your surprise!" Misses Chiles said as she was walked toward Mister Chiles. "And Malcolm, send Faith home!"

With that, Malcolm took off running and fast as he could. The farm dogs ran fast behind him, barking with excitement. Dust flew in the air and the chickens scattered about, squawking as they fled.

Misses Chiles turned to Mister Chiles and cupped his face in her hands. With tears in her eyes, she said, "That boy is running to troubled times."

The closer Malcolm got to the cabin, the slower he ran. He could see the light beaming from the windows and smoke from the chimney, but he knew more waited for him behind those doors. *What did Misses Chiles mean when she said "unexpected visitor?"* he wondered. The statement made him hesitate, so he paused. Malcolm walked toward the wooden front door, and slowly pushed it open.

Hearing the door open, Faith stood and put her fingers to her lips in order to silence Malcolm. She reached out and took Malcolm's hand. She noticed that it was wet and sweaty, and seemed to be shaking. That made her smile.

Malcolm looked around his home, not even acknowledging Faith. He was trying to make out what was wrong. He saw Tulip laying on the bed, looking like a perfect sleeping angel. His heart skipped a beat. Tulip was becoming a beautiful woman right before his eyes. How he loved her.

Faith slowly guided Malcolm over to the cradle, where his baby daughter lay sleeping. Malcolm looked down at the baby, looked at Tulip, who was fast to sleep, and looked at Faith.

"This is your new daughter!" stated Faith with a rush of excitement. "Her name is Solo."

Malcolm looked down at the very white and pink little thing. "How? When?"

"Today, and I helped," Faith said proudly. "Isn't she beautiful?" she gushed, as if it was her own baby.

Malcolm continued to look at the baby and asked, "Why is the baby so white, with that golden hair? She looks like you, Faith."

Faith looked at Solo and knew that Malcolm was right, and she simply turned to Malcolm and repeated what her Mama had told her.

"Malcolm," said Faith with authority, "we colored folks come in different kinds of colors, just like flowers, and you know how much Tulip loves flowers." Faith was smiling. "Your daughter is just a different colored flower, just like me," she added proudly.

"Will she get darker?" Malcolm asked with concern.

"Maybe, I really don't know," replied Faith. "I didn't," she stated, annoyed at Malcolm's concerns about his daughter's skin color.

"What difference does it make? She's beautiful and she's your daughter," said Faith.

"Yep. That she is," said Malcolm. "But she's so little."

Faith laughed, "Yea, just born!"

"What did you say her name was? Solo?" asked Malcolm, looking puzzled.

"Yes," said Faith. "It's magical. Tulip named her that because she was inside her body all alone, without anyone knowing"

"Faith," says Malcolm suddenly remembering his wife. "How is Tulip? Is she going to be okay having the baby so fast and all?"

Faith laughed and recalled that the colored midwife said that she was right on time, with not a minute to spare.

Faith gathered her things and looked at Malcolm. "Go to your wife. She is going to need you when she wakes up. Mama said overnight, the baby will need feeding, so just give her to Tulip when she wakes up, and she will know what to do," Faith said, smiling. "Also, make sure to check her for wetness. In the cradle are extra changing clothes and pins, and don't let the baby stay wet long," cautioned Faith. "If so, she will make a lot of noise, and we need to let Tulip get some rest."

Malcolm felt overwhelmed with so many instructions. He just wanted to get in the bed and be close to Tulip. He didn't know anything about changing babies, and didn't want to learn. As Faith opened the door, she called out, "Maw left grub on the stove for your supper. Please make sure Tulip eats a little. She needs to get her strength and nourishment to feed the baby. I'll be back to help Tulip in the morning, so goodnight, Malcolm. I am so happy for you and Tulip."

Faith closed the door with Malcolm standing in the middle of the cabin floor. Malcolm wondered how Faith got so grown.

Malcolm slowly walked over to Tulip and sat on the bed. He stroked the hair from Tulip's face.

Tulip opened her eyes and focused on Malcolm's face. Tears came to her eyes. "I'm sorry, Malcolm."

"Sorry for what? She's beautiful, just like her Mama."

"But she is so white, and did you see her eyes?" Tulip asked apologetically.

"Yea, she is very white," said Malcolm, looking worried.

"Misses Chiles says colored babies are born sometimes light because of our race being all mixed up, and that we come in all colors, like flowers," Tulip said in a rushed voice as she rose to embrace Malcolm. "She is yours, Malcolm. She's yours."

"Why are you talking crazy, Tulip? I know that, but what's with that name? Solo?" They both laughed, but not too loudly. They didn't want to wake their baby.

"Solo, didn't I tell you to stay put?" said Tulip.

Solo was now two years old was as busy as a possum. Tulip found it impossible to keep up with the gray-and-blue-eyed beauty. She was always getting into stuff and wandering off into the woods. Tulip found it hard to run after her, since she was expecting another baby any day now. If it wasn't for Faith, who simply adored Solo, she didn't know how she would get her chores done and have Malcolm's supper ready for when or if he got home. It seemed that Malcolm was getting home later and later, and sometimes, not at all. Tulip realized that there was an extra mouth to feed and another on the way, and that Malcolm needed to make extra money. They also wanted to put a little away so they could buy their own little farm. But Malcolm had taken to drinking and staying away from home. He didn't spend any time with Solo and very little time with Tulip.

As time went by, Solo didn't get darker. She stayed white with the gray-blue eyes and hair that was thick, curly, and yellow as the sun. Many folks thought she was another of Misses Chiles's youngins.

"Solo, I am not going to call you anymore," said Tulip, trying not to smile. *This girl is a handful,* thought Tulip. Solo came running to her Mama, giggling along the way.

"Mama, Mama, come," Solo said in her baby voice.

"No," said Tulip, "Mama wants you to come to her. Now sit here while I put the plates on the table. Your Papa will be home soon, and we want to have everything ready for him."

"Pap Pap," said Solo while smiling and clapping her hands.

Tulip looked at her daughter and thought, *If only your Pap Pap felt the same way.*

Since the Solo's birth, things had changed between Tulip and Malcolm. Malcolm knew of colored families with mixed children. Even the Chileses were a mixed family, and he had no problem with that. But Malcolm knew that he was not from a mixed family. His father, mother, grandparents, uncles, and aunts were all colored folks.

He still didn't know enough about Tulip's kin. There had to be some mixing with white folks along the way. If not, how could he account for Solo, his daughter? Tulip said that she had never been with anyone before him, and that there had been no mixing in her family. But even though Solo was as cute as a button and Malcolm had feelings for her, she didn't look like him or her mother or kin.

It was hard for Malcolm to accept Solo. Often, he would just push her away, so he tried to stay away from home until she was asleep. But now, Tulip was with child again. Malcolm wondered if this one would be like Solo. *If I'm going to have youngins, I want them to look like me. Dammit, I need a drink.*

"Hey, Malcolm," said Tulip, kneeling before the fire stove. "I didn't hear you come in."

"Pap Pap!" yelled Solo, her arms outstretched to get her Papa's attention.

Malcolm looked in Solo's direction but didn't respond to her calling him.

Solo gave her Papa a big smile.

Malcolm felt guilty about not acknowledging Solo. She was just a baby, and it wasn't her fault. But that still didn't quiet his nagging doubt.

"You home early. Is everything okay?" asked Tulip.

"Yeah," said Malcolm.

Since Solo's birth, most of Tulip and Malcolm's conversations were short, and sometimes just one word. While the sex didn't stop completely, the lovemaking had. Malcolm was quick with Tulip, and didn't make eye contact. Now Tulip found herself with child, but at least this time, she knew it was in there, as well as how it got there.

"'Yeah,' 'no,' 'hungry,' 'fine,' 'tired,' 'good morning'..." Tulip repeated in rapid succession, hoping that Malcolm could sense her unhappiness.

Malcolm just looked at his wife and gave no response. Unlike her pregnancy with Solo, Tulip was very big, according to Dr. Foster. Even he had taken an interest in Tulip after her fainting incident in town. After Solo's birth, Dr. Foster came out to the Chiles's farm to inspect the baby. He was taken aback at the baby's beauty, and clearly recognized that she was of mixed lineage, which wasn't uncommon among those parts.

In his practice, Dr. Foster would run across colored girls in the family way. After the birth of a mulatto, some would insist that they had not been with a white man, and some were silent. As with Misses Chiles, some of the mixed babies were sent away to live with other relatives, or some were given to childless white families.

Tulip had suppressed the memory of the terrible assault and violation she experienced at the Betts's farm. With the absence of this memory, in her mind, she'd only had sex with her husband. But Solo's birth had proven that that wasn't the case.

Folks who met Solo couldn't resist her gray-blue eyes and curly blond hair. Tulip was careful not to let too many menfolk touch Solo, especially, white men. Solo had a smile that would light up her little dimpled face. She loved music and would shake with the rhythm of any type of music. Solo would smile and be sweet to get her way, but Tulip knew that Solo wasn't so sweet when she didn't.

When it came to his daughter, Malcolm wished he didn't have the nagging feeling that she wasn't his. Just as bad, he was tired of folks—both men and women—teasing him about what they thought about Tulip. They would say things like he was stupid for marrying her, and that Solo wasn't his but some white man's. They said Tulip tricked him into marrying her. Such talk outraged Malcolm. He drank more and stayed away from home. Malcolm had even gotten into fights with men who said bad things about his wife. Some would say that Tulip was too good to f—k them, but would f—k a white man. Some girls and even grown women flirted with Malcolm openly, and said that they knew Tulip was a slut. Sometimes it was hard for Malcolm to resist offers of sex, especially after a few drinks. But he loved Tulip, and just wanted to know the truth.

One day, he confessed his feelings about his baby daughter to Mister Chiles. While Mister Chiles was sympathetic to Malcolm's feelings, he told him to talk to his wife and be open about his feelings, and not to be so hard on Solo, because it wasn't her fault. Malcolm appreciated Mister Chiles's advice, but when he tried to talk with Tulip about his feelings, especially when it came to Solo, Tulip would get upset. Malcolm felt that it was best to leave things be and move on. Solo was his daughter. So be it. She was there, and there was nothing no one could do about it. In his gut, however, he felt that something wasn't right.

Now another baby was on the way. *What if this one looked like Solo?* The rage built up within Malcolm's gut and traveled through his insides, making him feel as if he would burst. His home was no longer a happy place to him.

"Pap Pap!" called out Solo.

They intertwined with our very soul,
mixing our heritage to be unrecognizable.
Mothers cry, fathers would deny.
The product, children, now must survive.
How dare they, the world would say,
but they could, and they did, so here we are;
a mixed bag of nothing, so they thought.
But, that was not to be, because the lineage that was created within
made us who we were destined to be.
No shame, no hate,
but yet we must endure constant shame and pain.
Not by choice, but certainly by force.
So mixed-up, not of a pure one.
But we stand tall, and not hide by the invisible wall of shame.
Who's to blame?

chapter twenty-seven

Identity

Years went by like seasons in the wind. Tulip and Malcolm now had three little ones underfoot, and their cabin was getting mighty crowded. Tulip and Malcolm had hoped to have moved on from the Chiles's farm by this time, but with the babies coming so fast, that didn't happen. As a young man, this was very frustrating for Malcolm. He felt that life was passing him by.

Solo was now six. Little Henry was four and was the spitting image of his father, with a smile that would light up the world. Then there was Baby Cecila, who was two and by far the hardest one to bring into the world for Tulip. The old colored midwife told Tulip that, even though Tulip was still a young woman at twenty-two, there would be no more children: she'd suffered too much damage to her womb. The midwife had seen that before, too, and shook her head sadly.

Tulip didn't explain to Malcolm that she could not birth anymore babies. In all honesty, she wasn't mad about it. Birthing babies was hard and painful, and who needed that? Still, Tulip secretly wished that their firstborn looked like the other two—not that she loved Solo any differently from the other children, but it was just different to have a child that looked nothing like her Mama or Papa. Solo was still blond, pale, and had those gray-blue eyes. On stop of that, she was as stubborn as a mule, with a temper to match, which made her Papa furious.

Sometimes, Tulip regretted the day Solo was born, which made Tulip feel guilty and ashamed. Tulip had noticed the change in Malcolm since Solo's birth. He was always questioning her about Solo's looks or accusing her of being with another man before him. She knew Malcolm didn't think Solo was his, but what could she say? He was her father. Malcolm was the first man Tulip loved.

Tulip and Malcolm argued and yelled often. Tulip would cry and Malcolm with storm out of the house and stay gone for days. Tulip missed her kind and sweet Malcolm. No longer did he smile and tease her. Their lovemaking was quick and rough. Malcolm even took to staying away from home longer, and when he did come home, he smelled of liquor.

Tulip had hoped that the other children, especially Little Henry, would make Malcolm happy. Tulip confided in Misses Chiles, who told her to be patient and understanding. But Malcolm remained distant, and Tulip didn't know how or if she could bring him back to her.

"Solo! Solo! Get down from that tree," yelled Malcolm.

Solo ignored him. Solo thought to herself, *He always yells at me and tells me what not to do. I can do what want. It doesn't matter what I do. He doesn't like me, anyway. I don't care, and I don't like him. When I grow up, I'm going to leave this place and then Papa will be sorry. I'm going to be a singer and a dancer.*

Solo defiantly began to sing aloud to block out the sound of her Papa calling her name. She hoped to make him mad.

"*Solo!*" Malcolm yelled. "I know she hears me!" Malcolm said out loud. "*Solo!*" Malcolm yelled again. *This girl has been nothing but trouble since the day she was born*, he thought. *Coming into this world looking like a white girl, no child of mine.*

Malcolm recalled that, when Solo was no more than two or three, he overheard her telling Faith, "I white like you." Malcolm had scolded her and told her that she was colored, not white.

Another time, he caught Solo holding her arm up against Little Henry and saying, "You are a n—r and I white." For that, Malcolm had whipped her good because he didn't want "n—r" said in his house, and his son would never be a "n—r," let alone to his own sister.

Malcolm understood that colored folk were mixed with whites in some form, but he didn't expect a child of his to be born white. She seemed to understand that she was different from her Mama and Papa. She seemed to prefer the Chileses over her own kin. Solo was downright disrespectful toward Malcolm, and she knew just how to push his buttons.

Many of Tulip and Malcolm's arguments were centered around Solo's behavior. Malcolm knew that Solo was a handful for Tulip. But Tulip sometimes thought that Malcolm was too hard on Solo and didn't believe Malcolm when he told her how Solo lied and pretended to be white.

Once, when Malcolm took Solo to town with him, he left Solo outside in the wagon while he went into the store to pick up the supplies. When he came back to the wagon, a few white folks had gathered around, telling her that she was pretty little girl, and Solo beamed under the praises. He overheard one white woman ask Solo her name, and fully aware that her Papa was listening, proudly said, "My name is Solo Chiles." She looked at her Papa and smiled.

One of the white women said, "Oh, you're Judith Chiles's daughter! I knew your Mama when she a little girl. Pretty little thing, just like you." The white women walked away, whispering among themselves and sneaking glances at the child.

The lie really bothered Malcolm, and on the road home, he asked her, "Why did you lie and tell those ladies that your name was Chiles?"

Solo looked at him. "Because you said I'm not your child, and I don't know any other name than Chiles."

Malcolm could have died right on the spot. From that day, he knew that Solo did not think that he was her Papa, and Malcolm didn't really see the need to convince her otherwise.

Malcolm realized that Solo was just a child, and because of his love for his family, he tried his best to hold in his feelings and move on. But between the constant teasing from his friends, Solo's outright disrespect, and Tulip's growing resentment, Malcolm felt as if a storm was slowly brewing over his head.

"*Solo!*" Malcolm yelled.

Solo figured she had made him mad enough. She began to climb down the large oak tree. She loved sitting in the tree, from where she could look out around the farm. It made her feel special, being up that high above everyone and everything.

"Yes, Papa, I'm coming," Solo replied.

By this time, Malcolm had worked himself up to a frenzy. He roughly grabbed her by the arm and began hitting her backside as she tried to pull away. "Didn't you hear me calling you?" Malcolm screamed. Solo tried to pull away, and cried out.

"Sorry, Papa, but I didn't hear you! I'm sorry!" Solo cried. He hit her harder, pulling her arm toward him as she tried to pull away. This tug of war went on for minutes.

"My arm, Papa!" cried out Solo. "You're hurting my arm! *Please stop!*" she cried out louder.

"If you stop pulling away from me, your arm wouldn't hurt!"

Malcolm yelled in anger and frustration.

Solo screamed so loud that Misses Chiles heard her from down the path. Misses Chiles came running with the younger children, Charity and Hope. Faith was now married off to Ben.

Tulip also heard the screaming and yelling, but it was nothing new to her. Malcolm and Solo always seemed to have some kind of ruckus going on. But Tulip thought it best to stop it before someone got hurt, and one day, it may not be Solo. She grabbed Baby Cecila and walked in the direction of Solo's screaming. Little Henry was quickly on her heels.

"What is all the ruckus?" demanded Misses Chiles as she looked between Malcolm and Solo. Malcolm seemed to have lost his senses. It wasn't Misses Chiles's way to intervene when Tulip and Malcolm whipping their children, even though she didn't like it. Over the years, she had watched Malcolm around Solo, so she knew very well that Malcolm was not that fond of his daughter, and for reasons Misses Chiles understood personally. But she didn't like the beatings, and she didn't want see Malcolm do something he would regret, even though she knew that Solo could be a handful.

"Malcolm!" He was so caught up in his emotions, he didn't realize how badly he was hurting Solo, nor did he hear Misses Chiles calling out his name. Finally Misses Chiles got Malcolm's attention, and he saw Tulip approaching him with a horrid look on her face.

Malcolm slowly released Solo and she fell to the ground, crying out and clutching her injured arm. First, Malcolm just stared at her like he was trying to decide what to do. Finally, he knelt down and reached for his sobbing daughter, but Solo scooted away from him on the ground like a frightened rabbit escaping capture.

Misses Chiles and Tulip ran to comfort Solo, as it was obvious she was hurt. Tulip was carrying Baby Cecila, who was looking more and more like a little version of her Mama. Misses Chiles picked up Solo, who was very small for six. Solo was crying, and her injured arm hung limp. Misses Chiles had seen enough broken bones in her time to know that Solo's arm was fractured. "Malcolm, how could you? She's just a child," scolded Misses Chiles. "Shame on you!"

Malcolm could not make eye contact with Misses Chiles. Sweat covered his face. He felt Tulip's eyes burn into his soul, but he would not look at her. He hung his head and walked away without saying a word. All eyes were on him, except Solo, who was weeping into Misses Chiles's breast. As Malcolm walked away, he felt a little hand nestle into his. He looked down and saw Little Henry looking up at him.

Misses Chiles carried Solo to her home. She told Tulip to clear the supper table, and then she gently placed Solo on the wood surface.

Solo's little face was pink and stained from crying. She looked up at Misses Chiles with her pretty gray and blue eyes. "Papa hurt my arm. He is mean."

Misses Chiles thought her heart would burst. The moment took her back to a time when she was about Solo's age and she was hurt by kin. At that moment, she knew that life would be hard for Solo. "Hush now, baby girl. Your Papa didn't mean no harm, and he sorry that he hurt you," Misses Chiles said lovingly. "You know, Solo, menfolk are big and strong, and sometimes, they don't know their own strength."

"Yes, Papa does!" yelled Solo, which took Misses Chiles by surprise.

"Solo, mind your manners!" yelled Tulip.

"Papa hates me because I don't look like Little Henry and Baby Cecila," said Solo, with tears streaming down her face. "He thinks

I'm white!" cried Solo.

"Now, stop such nonsense," said Misses Chiles. "Your Papa loves you, he just has a different way of showing it."

Solo screamed, "I hate him, I hate him!"

"Don't you ever repeat such foolishness," Tulip said. "You are your Papa's child, just like your brother and sister. He feeds you, protects you, puts a roof over your head. Don't you ever use that 'hate' word. You mind your manners and let Misses Chiles tend to your arm."

Solo and Tulip's eyes locked, and the house was silent. At that moment, an understanding between mother and daughter was formed, and only time would tell what that was.

Dreams deferred, love astray,
we both wondered when it did all go away;
Together we talked, we had hopes, we prayed,
we even put our reality into play;
Like seasons in time, blowing wind, falling snow,
flying birds, our love strayed;
We reached out in fright, trying to regain,
hoping somehow to recover our lost;
I love you, you say, I love you, I say,
but it is now not meant in any special way;
What happened to the love
that we promised to each forever and a day!

chapter twenty-eight

Conflicts and Struggles

*M*onths passed after the incident between Solo and her Papa. Malcolm avoided his daughter and ignored her attempts to engage him. This usually left Solo in tears and running to the comfort of her Mama's arms. Tulip was so torn between the two, it was exhausting. She tried to explain to Solo that her Papa was sorry that he hurt her arm, and that he was sad. But Solo wasn't having it, and would stomp her foot in defiance and pout that her Papa hated her. Tulip scolded Solo for saying such things about her Papa, and warned Solo not to repeat such hurtful lies.

While Tulip felt bad for Solo, she felt worse for her husband, and feared she was losing him. Malcolm was staying away from their home for longer periods of time, and when he was home, he didn't bed Tulip or play with the children. Little Henry would grab his Papa around the legs, but Malcolm would only pat him on the head. Malcolm said very few words and made very little eye contact. Tulip would try to engage him in conversation, but he wouldn't respond. To Tulip, he always appeared deep in thought, like he had something heavy on his mind. She knew Malcolm struggled with his acceptance of Solo because she didn't look like the other children. But like Misses Chiles said, colored folks come in all colors. Tulip had come to understand that Malcolm didn't believe that Solo was his daughter, and that scared her.

Malcolm was conflicted and felt so much internal rage. He struggled with the acceptance of Solo as his daughter. He had come to believe that Tulip had tricked him: she had pretended to be an innocent little girl and seduced him, knowing all along that she had been with another man, possibly a white man, and was with child. She played him like a fool. It was very clear every time he looked at Solo. What happened that day when they were in town and she went running off like a crazed woman? Why did she cry out at night and sometimes fight him off when he tried to touch her?

Now Malcolm was putting the pieces together. Tulip's Paw was moving away because she was with child and he had to take her away. Malcolm thought, *From the looks of Solo, it was probably some white boy trash. How could she?* He had just lost his Paw. Tulip knew he was weak. She took advantage of his sadness and for that, he would never forgive her. She was a liar and nothing about their life was truth, except Little Henry and Baby Cecila. *How can I stay here under these lies?*

"Malcolm, Malcolm," called out Tulip. "I've been calling you. Didn't you hear me?" Tulip stood over Malcolm, who was sitting at the supper table with his hands in his head.

"Sorry," Malcolm said slowly, as if he was in a daze, but without making eye contact with Tulip.

Solo and Little Henry looked on between their Mama and Papa.

Solo asked, "Papa, are you sick?"

Malcolm shook his head no.

"Are you sad because you broke my arm?" Solo went on, secretly trying to make her Papa feel bad.

"Solo!" yelled Tulip, "Shut it before you don't get any supper."

"But, Mama, I was just asking," Solo cried.

"Stop that crying right now," Tulip said slamming her hands down on the hard wood supper table, rattling the plates and causing Baby Cecila to cry out from her cradle.

"Now look what you made me do!" yelled Tulip. She walked over to comfort Baby Cecila.

Malcolm didn't make a move or utter a word. He slowly rose from the table and walked out the front door. Tulip watched the door close and stood there contemplating what to do next. It seemed like an eternity went by, but in reality, it was only a few minutes.

"This got to stop," Tulip said to herself. She grabbed her sweater and ran toward the door. Turning back and as calmly as she could muster, she ordered, "Solo, fix your brother his supper, fix your plate, and then eat. I need to check on your Papa. Give Baby Cecila a bottle if she fusses. *You heard me?*" Tulip yelled with such force that it made the children jump in fright. They were not used to their Mama yelling.

Solo, knowing it was not the time for tantrums, nodded in acknowledgement.

It was a dark and cold night. The trees were still and there were only a few stars in the sky. As Tulip looked down the path, she didn't see any signs of Malcolm. The horses and buggy were still in place. He couldn't have gone far on foot, Tulip reasoned. Tulip called out Malcolm's name, but he didn't answer. Tulip walked down the path further and called out to Malcolm. Still no answer. This made Tulip both mad and frightened.

"Malcolm, please answer me!" Tulip cried out. "Please, I need you! I love you, Malcolm! Please, where are you?" Tulip continued to plead.

Drizzles of rain hit Tulip's head, but she walked on through the woods, calling out her husband name. It had been years since Tulip felt such abandonment and old feelings were coming full surface.

Tulip began to cry and fell to the ground. "Malcolm, please, please don't leave me! Malcolm, please!" Tulip cried.

Malcolm stood hidden in the dark of night. He heard his wife's cries, and her pleas tugged at his heart. But his feet would not move toward her.

While he could see her, he visualized the girl that he fell in love with—now the woman, his wife, the mother of his children. But he did not answer her, and he could not move. He was being pulled in two directions: stay or go?

Tears rolled down Malcolm's face. He looked to the sky for a sign. Finally, Malcolm saw her. He watched as Tulip fell to her knees and cried out for him. He felt as though his heart would explode. He loved her still, but he couldn't stay right now. He had to go. Malcolm walked farther into the woods. He wouldn't take the horses or wagon, because they belonged to the Chileses. He only had the clothes he was wearing, but his load was heavy.

Suddenly, Malcolm stopped as he heard Tulip cry out to him. His hands balled into tight fists. He gritted his teeth, put his head down, and sped up.

Tulip heard the rustle in the woods, and she ran in the direction of the noise. "Malcolm! Malcolm! Malcolm! Malcolm!" She yelled repeatedly. Tulip felt like she was going mad. She ran through the woods, stumbling along the way. The brushes tore at her dress and tree limbs hit her face, but she ran on, calling out to her husband. "Mama, Mama, where are you? I need to smell the flowers. Help me, Mama, I need you," she cried out.

She allowed herself to drift into the beautiful field of colorful lilies, roses, and tulips. Tulip walked slowly through the flowers, gently touching them as she went by. She felt at peace. In the distance, she saw a lone figure. *Could it be?* Tulip felt happy. *Mama! I'm here!* Tulip called out, waving her hand.

The lone figure waved back at Tulip, but as she got closer to the figure, the figure seemed to move farther away. Tulip called out, "Don't leave me, I need you!"

The woods were quiet, and the animals listened to the heartbreak of a human.

After supper, Solo had cleaned the plates and helped Little Henry put on his nightshirt. She and Little Henry looked out the window for their Mama and Papa, but it was too dark to see anything. Finally, Little Henry fell asleep, while Solo stayed by the window. She had heard her Mama calling for her Papa, but now she didn't hear anything, and it was quiet and dark. *It's all Papa's fault that Mama left,* thought Solo. "I hope he doesn't come back, ever," she said aloud. "I hate him."

When Solo awoke in the morning, the fire had died out, and neither Mama nor Papa were in the house.

Solo walked down the path to the Chiles's house with Baby Cecila on her little hip and Little Henry towing behind her. Misses Chiles saw the children approaching. She stopped hanging the clothes on the line and looked towards them. *This is strange,* she thought to herself. *Where are Tulip and Malcolm?*

"Oh my God!" Fear rushed through to her as she wondered what had happened. Misses Chiles dropped her wash and ran toward the children, while her own children looked on.

"Solo!" called Misses Chiles, "My child, what in God's name are you children doing out here? Where's your Mama?"

Solo walked toward Misses Chiles and tried to explain what had happened the night before.

Misses Chiles took the children to her home and told them to stay put. Mister Chiles had already left for work, and she thought that perhaps Malcolm was with him. But where was Tulip? "Solo, stay here with the children, while I go find your Mama."

"Is my Mama hurt?" Solo asked, nearly in tears.

"Papa was mean to her," Solo went on. "He made her cry," she lied.

Misses Chiles didn't respond. Since the incident with Solo, Misses Chiles knew that all was not right with Tulip and Malcolm. She and Mister Chiles saw the change in Malcolm. Misses Chiles had even asked her husband to talk to him. She had prayed that Malcolm would just accept his family, but she knew in her heart that a storm was coming.

Misses Chiles walked back toward Tulip and Malcolm's cabin. She called out to Tulip, but there was no answer. She noticed that the buggy and horses were still there, so that Tulip and Malcolm must be on foot. Misses Chiles looked in the house and saw the remains of the prior night's supper on the stove and an empty fireplace.

As she walked toward the woods, she heard a muffled sound. Misses Chiles called out to Tulip. Fear gripped her. *What if Malcolm hurt Tulip?*

"Tulip!" she called out, with no answer. Misses Chiles continued to move slowly and listened for any sound. Just ahead of her, she saw Tulip laying against a stump.

She rushed toward Tulip. "Tulip, my dear, are you hurt? My dear, are you hurt?" Misses Chiles pleaded.

Tulip slowly opened her red, glassy, cloudy eyes and looked at Misses Chiles. Tulip's face was stained with dirt and dried tears. She was wet from the morning dew. She looked like a wounded lost animal. Misses Chiles's heart went out to her. She gathered Tulip in her arms, and the two women just held on.

The heart knows when love goes cold,
with no way to bring back the old;
From the start, we lived life as if we were one, the fun, the
moments, the endless passion could not be outdone;
Our love was real, spoken, and new,
but how were we to know that was so untrue.

chapter twenty-nine

Searches of the Heart

In the light of the day, with chores to be done and children to care for, there is no time fret over what was gone. But in the dark of night, lost love, deferred dreams, and sorrow prevailed.

In the passing weeks after Malcolm left, Tulip moved through her days without any sense of consciousness. She woke up, got the children ready, fixed food, did the chores, and went to bed. She didn't visit the Chileses and they let her be. She didn't care about her hair, bathing, or clothing.

Nights were awful. Tulip dreamt of hands touching her body, violations, and her Secret being poked and rammed. There were flashes of unknown but familiar faces, and blood, so much blood. Tulip would wake up sweating and shaking. This recurring dream was adding to her despair. She missed Malcolm consoling her when she had these bad dreams.

Tulip replayed conversations in her mind as she struggled to understand Malcolm's absence. He was always asking questions about her family and wanting more details than she had to give. While she was sorry for lying about Mister Man being her Papa, she still couldn't piece together everything to explain the truth about Mister Man and the Bettses.

Is that what this is about? Did he leave because of Solo?

Tulip thought so much about the "whys" and "whats," she started having unyielding headaches. One minute, she assumed Malcolm walked away because he didn't believe Solo was his child and the next minute, she was worried about him being lost and hurt without a way to get back home. The worst pains came from thoughts of him simply leaving to escape her and the children and to be with another woman.

Tulip realized that many weeks had passed, and still no Malcolm. It was possible that he had come down with some sickness—there was a lot of that going around. She contemplated looking for him, but she couldn't just leave the children and run around looking for a grown man. *Besides,* Tulip thought, *where would I look?* Maybe he was with Jessie, or just needed a little time. Misses Chiles said that menfolk get little overwhelmed sometimes with working hard, and as good wives, now and then, women need to give them a little time to themselves. Misses Chiles said that Malcolm would come home, because they all do.

But what if he didn't? What about the children? Tulip knew that Malcolm wouldn't want her begging from the Chileses. They had their own family. What would she do without Malcolm? That thought alone would cause tears to roll down Tulip's face. Tulip had so many questions and no real answers. She was lost. She needed Malcolm to come home. *Now.*

Baby Cecila was too young to know what was going on. Tulip found comfort in her, with Cecila looking like her Mama.

Tulip knew that it was hard for Little Henry not to have his Papa home, especially with his Mama being sad and always crying. Little Henry tried to make his Mama happy. He would hug Tulip tightly around her waist, but she never hugged him back. Her arms just hung loosely by her side.

Little Henry missed his Papa and was scared without him. He needed his Papa. Deep in his heart, he blamed his sister Solo for Papa leaving. Solo was so sassy and bad, and she had been mean toward him since Papa left. He would tell Mama, but she just stared. Little Henry hoped his Papa would come home soon, so Mama would be happy again. He thought if only he wasn't so little, he could go look for his Papa. Every morning, when he opened his eyes, he looked around expecting to see his Papa sleeping next to his Mama. At night, Little Henry would sit by the window, hoping to see his Papa walk up the path. Sometimes, when everyone was asleep, he would cry. He didn't want anyone to see him crying during the day, he just watched and waited.

On the other hand, Solo was her happy-go-lucky self. She appeared not to have a care in the world. She didn't appreciate having to take care of Baby Cecila, however, because Mama was always crying or just sitting around. Solo didn't think it fair that she had to do all the work now that mean Papa had run off. Her time to sing and dance was cut short. When she would sneak off to Misses Chiles's house, hoping to play with Hope or Charity, Misses Chiles would send her home. She told Solo that her Mama needed her help more until their Papa came home. There was no time to play. This made Solo mad and she would stomp down the path back home.

It was all Papa's fault that she couldn't have fun anymore. Even though she was glad that her Papa was gone, his leaving had made everything worse for her. Mama had stopped combing Solo's hair, which was fine with her because now she could wear her hair the way she wanted, like Faith wore hers, all piled up on top of her head.

Solo helped prepare supper as best she could. Then there were potatoes and vegetables to be picked, chickens to feed, eggs to be gathered, clothes to be washed, and more. To Solo, her Mama looked so ugly, moping around and crying all the time. She secretly wished her Mama would leave and then she could live with Misses Chiles.

Tulip sat at the supper table and watched the children eat. So far, there was plenty of meat, beans, and vegetables, but Tulip worried about the future. *What if Malcolm didn't come back?* Tulip thought. *What will happen to us?*

"Mama," Solo called out, breaking Tulip's thoughts.

"Yes, Solo?"

"Are you going to eat?"

Tulip looked down at the food growing cold on her plate, but she just couldn't bring herself eat it. "Yes, child. I'm going to eat."

"When?" Solo persisted.

Tulip looked up at her daughter.

"You never eat anymore!" yelled Solo. "You are going to die and leave us all alone. Just like Papa left!"

"Stop it, Solo!" Little Henry said in his small voice. "Leave Mama alone!"

"She's going to die if she doesn't eat, and what will happen to us?" Solo asked out loudly.

Little Henry didn't have the answer, so he just went back to eating his food and watching his Mama.

"Solo, I am not going to die," Tulip said softly. "I'm just not hungry right now, but I'll eat if that will stop you from yelling."

Solo just stared at her Mama and hoped that her Mama wouldn't eat and would just die.

A few weeks later, as Tulip lay in her bed with Baby Cecila close to her, she listened to the night sounds and noises coming from Solo and Little Henry. Her son reminded her so much of Malcolm. Even his sleeping sounds were like his Papa's. He was always so protective of her and watched her when he thought that she wasn't looking.

Tulip was grateful that Malcolm had taken time with Little Henry, showing him little things. Even though he was a little boy, he helped out as much as he could, trying to fill his father's shoes. Her heart went out to her sweet son because she knew he missed his Papa as much as she did.

Waiting for Malcolm to come home was driving her crazy, and she wasn't taking care of herself. In a way, Solo was right. Something had to change.

Solo rubbed her eyes and closed them quickly, because the sun was so bright. She looked around the cabin and saw that Mama was cooking. Plates were on the supper table. Solo had to take another look at her Mama because she had combed her hair and a put on one of her good dresses. Solo nudged Little Henry, attempting to wake him up.

"Stop, Solo," Little Henry said sleepily. "Leave me be."

Solo whispered in Little Henry's ear, "Wake up and look at Mama."

Little Henry sat up, rubbed his eyes, looked at his Mama, and smiled. He turned to Solo and said, "I told you Mama wasn't going to die."

"Come children, get up. You got to get a move on," said Tulip.

"Why, Mama? What's going on?" asked Solo.

Tulip turned in the direction of her daughter. "Solo, I will not have any mess from you today. Now get your butt up, wash your face, get dressed, and come and eat!"

Solo opened her mouth to object, but seeing the fiery look in her Mama's eyes, she decided against it. When the children were dressed and seated to eat, Tulip said very calmly, "Mister and Misses Chiles will be watching you all for a while, except for Baby Cecila. She will stay with Faith and Ben."

"No, I want to live with Faith!" screamed Solo.

Losing her patience, Tulip yelled, *"You stop it right now! I will not have any foolishness from you today! Finish your food!"*

Solo was furious, but she dared say no more. She thought to herself that she would find a way to live with Faith.

Little Henry wanted to ask his Mama where she was going, but he thought it was best not to.

Earlier that week, Tulip had gone to visit Misses Chiles. It had almost been two months since she found Tulip crumpled in the woods, crying out for Malcolm.

Mister Chiles told his wife that it was best to give Tulip some time, and let her come to them when she was ready. In town, Mister Chiles had spoken to Jessie and some other town folks who knew Malcolm. Talk was that Malcolm was taking on odd jobs on farms, and on some occasions, he would be out drinking and having his way with some of the local women. Mister Chiles learned that, after a while, Malcolm had left for the big city, New York. Jessie said he tried to convince Malcolm to return home to his family, because Tulip was a beautiful woman and his children needed him. But Malcolm just walked away.

From what Misses Chiles gathered from her husband, she knew Malcolm was gone, and probably wouldn't return. She was well aware of men deserting their families, and it made her sad, but at the same time, she felt blessed. *Thank God Noel was not one of those men.*

Tulip needed to know that her husband may never return, but Misses Chiles felt that it wasn't her place to convey that message. Concern about Tulip and the children's welfare had consumed Misses Chiles—a feeling that she shared with Faith, who was equally concerned. Misses Chiles would give Tulip time, but because Tulip and the children were kin, they needed to be checked on. When

Mister Chiles was away, she would sneak peaks at Tulip picking potatoes or washing. Sometimes, she would let the girls play with Solo and Little Henry. When her children returned from playing, she questioned them about how Solo and Little Henry were coming along. Of course, they said fine, which was even more frustrating. Because of this, when Tulip finally walked through Misses Chiles door, Misses Chiles was floored and relieved.

No longer did Tulip have that sweet, girlish innocence. She looked aged, as if life had taken its toll. She had lost a lot of weight, her eyes were vacant, and with her hair pulled tightly in a bun, she looked even older. Her clothes hung loosely on her shrunken frame, contributing to her looking so sad. Tulip had transcended from a girl to a woman. Heartbreak would do that.

Misses Chiles had to fight back her tears. She gathered Tulip in her arms as the two women embraced.

"I need to go find Malcolm," rambled Tulip, as if she was talking to the wind. "I can't go on without knowing where my husband is or if he's coming back. I got to know that he is okay. I need him to tell me that he doesn't want us anymore. He can't just walk off and say nothing. It's not right. This waiting and worrying is driving me crazy. I can't be a good mother to the children. I'm having strange dreams. I can't eat." Tulip went on and Misses Chiles listened and nodded her head in agreement.

"What do you need me to do, Tulip?" Misses Chiles asked. "You and the children are family, and Mister Chiles and I are here to help. Please know that this your home, and you and the children are welcome to stay as long as you want to. There is no need to worry about your keep. It's not a handout, because you are kin. If you need to go and find your husband, then you should go, because not knowing and worrying will drive you crazy. You can leave the children with us. Faith will help out and we will make do.

"Go, Tulip. Go, and may God be with you," she said, as she gave Tulip another hug.

Two weeks after Tulip and Misses Chiles spoke, Tulip spent several nights packing and getting things ready for her journey. She was excited, but she still longed for Malcolm to come walking up the path. Tulip had not told Solo and Little Henry about her plans. She didn't want them getting their hopes up or fretting about her leaving.

Misses Chiles had discussed the plan with Mister Chiles, and he agreed that they should take care of the children until either Tulip or Malcolm returned. After talking to Jessie, Mister Chiles doubted that Malcolm would return, but he did not tell his wife about that. He didn't want to upset her any more.

Full from their big breakfast, Tulip and the children walked down the path to the Chiles's home. Tulip carried sacks of clothing, Solo carried Baby Cecila, and Little Henry pulled a wagon full of their belongings. Tulip didn't want to look back at the cabin, because it would only bring back the beautiful memories of Malcolm and their wedding night. Tulip kept her head up and looked ahead toward the Chiles's home.

Mister Chiles, Misses Chiles, Faith, Hope, Charity, Ben, and even Max were all waiting for their arrival. They watched as Tulip and the children approached them. Each was consumed with his or her own emotions.

Mister Chiles was proud of Little Henry trying to pull the heavy loaded wagon.

Misses Chiles could see the scowl on Solo's face, and shook her head.

Faith was sad that Tulip had experienced such heartbreak, but since she and Ben had struggled to conceive their own baby, they were excited about having Baby Cecila.

Tulip stopped and told the children to wait. She set down her bundles and approached the Chileses. Tulip walked toward Misses Chiles, took both her hands, and with tear-filled eyes, Tulip said, "Please look over my babies and let them know that their Mama and Papa love them. Baby Celica won't need much, just some kisses."

Tulip turned to Mister Chiles. "I know that you will watch over Little Henry and show him things." Mister Chiles nodded in agreement.

Tulip walked over to Faith and hugged her, and said, "I love you, dear sister."

"Thank you all for your help."

Tulip called to her children. She took Baby Cecila from Solo, who was relieved to get rid of her, and covered the baby's face with kisses. Baby Cecila giggled in delight. She handed her to Faith, who beamed.

"Take care of her."

Tulip walked back to Solo and Little Henry and knelt in the dirt before them. She took their hands, but Solo immediately pulled back. Tulip, ignoring Solo, reached out and took Little Henry in her arms.

"You are my little man. Watch out for your sisters and be respectful of Mister and Misses Chiles."

Little Henry, overcome with tears and emotion, feigned confidence. "I will, Mama," he said. "When will you be back? Will you bring Papa home?" he asked.

"I'll try," Tulip said, holding her son close. "Now, go to Mister Chiles."

Tulip put her arms out to Solo, who stepped back. "Solo, I want you be good and respectful. No sassing and talking back. You do as you're told. Now come and give your Mama a hug."

Solo stepped back again as her Mama reached for her. She stared at her Mama with resentment. "*I want to live with Faith!*" she screamed.

Trying to hold her temper, Tulip stood up and looked down at Solo. "Solo, we already talked about that, so stop your yelling and come give me a hug."

"No! I hate you and I hope you never come back, like Papa!" Solo yelled as she ran back toward their cabin.

Faith handed Baby Cecila to her Mama and told Tulip that she would go after Solo. Tulip watched as her blond hair little girl went running down the dirt path.

Mister Chiles and Little Henry had bought the horse and buggy around. Misses Chiles had asked her husband to take Tulip to town. Tulip would make her way from there. Mister Chiles picked up Tulip's bundles and tossed them into the wagon. "Ready, Tulip? We need to get going so I can get back before nightfall." Tulip nodded her head and ran to Misses Chiles.

Tulip, Misses Chiles and Baby Cecila were locked in a hug. The women were overcome with emotions. Little Henry ran up and hugged his Mama's backside. Tulip stroked Baby Cecila's head and kissed her. Silently, she mouthed "Thank you" to Misses Chiles. She turned and reached down to pick up Little Henry who hugged her tightly around her neck. Tulip carried him as she walked to the wagon. She smelled him and kissed his head. With that, she climbed up onto the buggy.

Misses Chiles handed Baby Cecila to Ben and walked over and picked up Little Henry. Mister Chiles turned and looked at his wife and said, "Be home soon."

Tulip sat straight up in the buggy as it proceeded down the road.

She knew that if she turned around, she would tell Mister Chiles to stop and run back to her children, so she never looked back.

Instead, she thought, *Malcolm, I'm coming.*

Come find me love, for I am lost,
for in the midst of my life, there is no movement;
For here is now and forever.
Things and times are growing away as I search for you;
No one seems to see the light of day or tears of rain for me;
it is all the same;
I wonder what is next in this time and place,
because without you it is like my very existence has gone.
I must find you.

TO BE CONTINUED…

SPECIAL ACKNOWLEDGMENTS

I wish to express my sincere love and gratitude to my daughter, Kary L. Perry, who believed in me, threatened me, and pushed me to make my dream a reality. Her support means more than she will ever know. But, equally as important, she connected me to the remarkably talented Renita Bryant, owner of Mynd Matters Publishing. She was so open, honest, and trusting that my fears disappeared. I am so very fortunate to have Renita publish my first novel and I'm certain this will be a lasting relationship.

I thank my husband, who never judges and always gives me support and confidence.

Finally, I thank every one of my readers. Just know, it will only get better.

Love you!